The Forest Brims Over

The Forest Brims Over

A NOVEL

Maru Ayase

Translated from the Japanese
by Haydn Trowell

COUNTERPOINT | BERKELEY

The Forest Brims Over
First Counterpoint edition: 2023

English translation copyright © 2023 by Haydn Trowell

Copyright © 2019 Maru Ayase

Original title: *Mori ga Afureru*
Original Japanese edition published by KAWADE SHOBO SHINSHA
Ltd. Publishers
English-language translation rights reserved to Counterpoint under
license granted by Maru Ayase arranged with KAWADE SHOBO
SHINSHA Ltd. Publishers

Library of Congress Cataloging-in-Publication Data
Names: Ayase, Maru, 1986- author. | Trowell, Haydn, translator.
Title: The forest brims over : a novel / Maru Ayase ; translated from the
 Japanese by Haydn Trowell.
Other titles: Mori ga afureru. English
Description: First Counterpoint edition. | Berkeley : Counterpoint,
 2023. | Original Japanese edition published by Kawade Shobo
 Shinsha Ltd. Publishers.
Identifiers: LCCN 2022060966 | ISBN 9781640095373 (trade
 paperback) | ISBN 9781640095380 (ebook)
Subjects: LCGFT: Novels.
Classification: LCC PL867.5.Y37 M6713 2023 | DDC 895.6—dc23/
 eng/20230302
LC record available at https://lccn.loc.gov/2022060966

Cover design by Dana Li
Cover art by Maki Ohkojima
Book design by Laura Berry

COUNTERPOINT
2560 Ninth Street, Suite 318
Berkeley, CA 94710
www.counterpointpress.com

Printed in the United States of America

10 9 8 7 6 5 4 3 2 1

The Forest Brims Over

1

WHEN HE GLANCED HER WAY, SEKIGUCHI
Masashi saw that the writer's wife, sitting at the
kitchen table, had started silently munching away
on a bowlful of mixed nuts. She was sucking them
into her mouth one after another, grains of every size
and color imaginable—brown, cream, black, white.
Sekiguchi felt a sticky sense of discomfort spread
throughout his chest just watching. He had never
had a strong stomach. A bowl of oil-rich nuts would
undoubtedly give him indigestion.

He was watching her over the shoulder of her husband, the author seated across from him, Nowatari
Tetsuya. The wife was slouched over with her cheek
pressed against the table, her hand moving back and
forth between the bowl and her mouth as she stared
across at him—or rather, at her husband's back.

"Hmm, well . . . How about a protagonist like
this then? A woman who unconsciously parrots the
words of everyone around her—her husband, her
children's classroom teachers, the owner of a bar she
frequents, you name it. She's completely vacuous,

without even the slightest sense of self, but that's the beauty of her. She has an innocence, a purity of mind like a delicate glass vessel, untainted by soiled ideas or thoughts. I wrote about the same kind of woman in my last short story, but I think it will have more impact in a novel-length work."

"Interesting. That certainly does sound like your style. A work filled with philosophical depth." Distracted by the wife's actions, Sekiguchi could provide only the vaguest of responses.

Nowatari cast his gaze to the glass ashtray in the center of the coffee table as he started mumbling to himself. "Hmm, and yet, hmm . . ."

The author looked like he was stewing over something. Nonetheless, Sekiguchi knew that if he were to speak up now, he would only find himself at the receiving end of a dark glower for having interrupted the writer's thoughts.

Nowatari was the kind of author who looked to his editor not for opinions or advice but simply for someone with whom to bounce ideas. To be honest, it would have made no difference whether it was Sekiguchi sitting across from him or a Jolly Chimp toy complete with banging cymbals. In a sense, he was a very hands-off writer, the kind who would sink into a sea of contemplation entirely by himself and would then put together a story of a certain quality without any outside intervention.

That was why Sekiguchi could turn his attention unreservedly to the wife. She spent close to twenty minutes quietly finishing the bowl of nuts and then went to retrieve a two-liter bottle of mineral water from the fridge. She poured the water into a glass, tilted her head back, and gulped it down in one swallow.

Then, in a single soft, slow motion, like a tree hacked from its roots, she fell flat to the floor.

"Ah," emerged a cry from Sekiguchi's throat.

Nowatari glanced over his shoulder before dashing into the kitchen a heartbeat later. "What's wrong, Rui?!"

The wife blinked heavily as her husband took her in his arms, and she casually pushed him away. "I'm a bit tired."

"What . . . ? If you need to get some sleep, go to bed first."

"Yes. I'll do that." The wife rose to her feet more surely than Sekiguchi would have expected.

"I'm sorry for disturbing you, Mr. Sekiguchi. Please, take your time." She flashed him a wry smile as she walked past.

With those parting words, she made her way out of the living room, probably to the bedroom on the second floor, as the pitter-patter of her light footsteps echoed down the staircase.

"What was all that about?" Nowatari frowned

before staring fixedly at the empty bowl on the kitchen table. "Is that . . . ?"

"Ah, your wife was having a bite to eat just now."

"She was eating *that*? You've got to be kidding me! I was going to plant those seeds in the empty plot next door!"

The author's face turned pale, and he sped upstairs, empty bowl in hand. "Rui, Rui!" he cried in a high-pitched wail, which was soon followed by his wife's low, ragged voice.

Holed up with his wife on the second floor, embroiled in heated discussion, Nowatari still hadn't returned even thirty minutes later. Sekiguchi, giving up on completing their meeting, scribbled a note to leave in the living room and set off back to the office.

NOWATARI TETSUYA AND his wife, Rui, were widely known in the publishing world as a pair of lovebirds.

Why was it that the wife, twelve years her husband's junior, was just as well known as he was? The answer to that question could be found in his breakthrough work.

Eight years earlier, the then-thirty-five-year-old author, who had already passed seven years since his literary debut, first entered the limelight when his novella *Tears*, a story that followed the invigorating romantic exchanges between a young man and woman, earned him his first-ever nomination for a prestigious prize. The text might have been a work of fiction, but not only was the Japanese title pronounced the same as his wife's name, it was also clearly grounded on his relationship with her.

When Sekiguchi met Rui for the first time at the Nowatari residence, a certain passage from *Tears* sprang to mind:

> *Her body, with her unadorned shorts and naked torso, reminded me of the little green peppers that I had fumbled with as a child in the fields under the blazing summer sun. That unaffected object, softly attenuated by shallow shadows flowing over its occasional swells, glowed with a sense of clear purity.*

Rui, with her short-cropped hair and her flat, boyish build, was the very image of the wife from that work. Her lush, dark eyes flickered with light as she gave him a wispy nod.

"Are you Tetsuya's new editor? It's a pleasure to meet you."

"Sekiguchi, from Yamairi Press. Please forgive the intrusion," he said, accepting her soft hand.

He could feel sweat beginning to bead down his

back as various passages from *Tears* flashed before his eyes.

The touch of a firm, smooth green pepper, the unexpected moisture and warmth of its folds and interior, the way that its hard, distant flesh seemed to unravel and ripen the more you looked at it. The images from *Tears* that she conjured up were sensual, uncomfortable even, and irresistibly arousing. It was difficult to meet her gaze.

Rui didn't even pretend to be bothered by this reaction, smoothly letting go of his hand and making her way toward the kitchen.

Even now, more than three years since their first encounter, Sekiguchi could still recall the shadow of her shoulder blades floating on the back of her white tank top. It was a strange, airy feeling, as of having shaken hands with a character in a fable.

AT NOON THE following day, the editorial department at Yamairi Press received a telephone call from Nowatari. The writer wanted to apologize to Sekiguchi for having left their meeting prematurely, said that he would get back in touch again after he had developed a more concrete idea for his next work, and confirmed in rough terms their next deadline.

Finally, in the same tone of voice that someone might use when announcing that they had at long last managed to post a set of documents that they had forgotten to send out, Nowatari said: "My wife has germinated."

"Huh?"

"I'm sorry about this, but can you come over now? I need you to buy some things from the home center nearby. I've already checked—they're in stock."

He wanted Sekiguchi to pick up a huge water tank that was over a meter in diameter, soil, and fertilizer.

His wife . . . ? Germs? Was she unwell?

That was terrible news. He must have been thinking of growing houseplants in the water tank to aid in her recovery. Sekiguchi had heard of something similar before—they were called aquaterrariums, or something like that. Perhaps her odd behavior the previous day had been born from the shock of her sudden illness?

At any rate, ever since his breakout hit *Tears*, Nowatari was a stable writer. His works were continuously being nominated for literary awards, and there was a steady stream of requests from television and film producers for their dramatization rights. Fifteen years had passed since his debut, and in the last few years in particular, his writing ability had matured, his stories taking on a perfect level of depth. Not only that, but he spoke now with the urgent tone of a man on the verge of a breakthrough with his next work. If they were going to ride this out, Sekiguchi realized, he couldn't afford to spoil the author's mood.

He completed his tasks for the afternoon, went to the home center, loaded the company car with the requested items, and made his way to the author's house. By then, it was early evening. A shadowy, de-saturated sky loomed over the world, a purple haze hanging above the streets. He didn't much care for this time of day—if he was ever going to be caught in a traffic accident, this was when it would happen.

Nowatari resided in a newly built two-story house in the suburbs of Tokyo and had recently purchased the empty plot next door at a discounted rate to enlarge his property. He and his wife lived by themselves, but apparently they were thinking toward the future, about eventually having children and preparing for old age, and so were planning to build an adjoining study on the empty plot. Sekiguchi parked his car on the still-vacant piece of land, strained himself hauling the water tank from the back seat, and carried it to the entrance of the building on a borrowed cart.

He rang the doorbell and waited, but there was no response.

"Mr. Nowatari! It's Sekiguchi!" he called out, but still there was no sign of anyone behind the door.

Maybe he should try calling his mobile? He lifted his hand and placed it on the door handle.

With a soft push, the handle turned and the door opened. Though shocked by this careless approach to home security, he set the water tank down on the floor of the entranceway and glanced around the dimly lit room.

It didn't look like the Nowatari couple was out. He could hear the sound of running water from farther back in the house.

"Excuse me . . . ," he called out before removing his shoes to take a look inside.

There was no sign of anyone on the ground floor in the kitchen or in the living room, where he had spoken with Nowatari the previous day. The door at the back of the kitchen, however, was ajar. He pushed it open, revealing a long, narrow corridor. The first door led to the toilet. Given the design of the building, the other doors probably led to the bathroom and laundry. It was at this point that he recognized the sound of running water as coming from a shower. There was a voice mixed into the gaudy thrum of water breaking into myriad tiny shards.

It was Nowatari.

"I told you, it isn't what you're thinking. She's just one of my students, and all I was doing was giving her some advice. She's thinking of submitting a work to the New Writer of the Year award. Yes, I was late home, and I'm sorry about that. But after class, all we did was wait back in the classroom while everyone else came and went and discussed her story. You saw the meeting I had with Sekiguchi yesterday, right? It was no different from that. This is ridiculous, getting all worked up over something so trivial."

Nowatari was talking in his usual intelligent and soft-spoken tone of voice. Rui's response, on the other hand, was unclear, drowned out by the sound of running water.

The two of them were bathing together. Clearly, Sekiguchi realized, he had come at an inopportune moment. Nonetheless, the other items that Nowatari had asked for were still in the car, so there was no point just standing around. He needed to let them know that he had arrived.

He made his way back to the kitchen, took a deep breath, and called out loudly: "Are you home, Mr. Nowatari? It's Sekiguchi! Sorry for letting myself in, but I've got those things you wanted!"

He craned his neck, trying to put as much energy into his voice as possible, pretending to not yet know where they were. Then, he gently returned the door leading from the kitchen back to its original half-open position.

This time, it sounded like he had made himself heard. The shower had stopped.

"Sorry, we're in here! I'll be out in a moment!"

Sekiguchi waited in the living room for a few minutes, until Nowatari entered fully dressed in a casual collared shirt and a pair of deep-colored denim trousers. He was barefoot.

"Sorry for taking so much of your time."

"Not at all. Where do you want the water tank?"

"In the bedroom. Give me a hand."

The two of them made their way to the front door, lifted the water tank from either side, and carried it upstairs to the bedroom. Feeling like a trespasser, Sekiguchi tried to keep his eyes from roaming, but he couldn't avoid catching a view of their bedroom. In the middle, there was just a plain double bed, completely featureless except for two dented pillows and an upturned comforter. Rather, what caught his attention were the three large bookcases lined up close to the bed. Each shelf was densely packed with books. As an editor at a publishing company, he felt an urge to steal a glimpse of the titles of those works. There were only a few so-called recreational books, the majority being volumes on modern history, contemporary art, politics, the customs of different societies throughout the world, and so forth—all no doubt reference material that Nowatari used when penning his stories.

After setting the water tank by the bed, Sekiguchi brought the large bags of soil and fertilizer from the car up to the bedroom in two batches. Nowatari spread the dark, damp soil at the base of the tank, then carefully mixed in a layer of fertilizer with his

14 Maru Ayase

hands. The fertilizer was a darker, more brownish shade than the soil and seemed to have pieces of wood and some sort of powder mixed in.

"That should about do it. Do you mind if I excuse myself for a moment? I'll just fetch my wife from the bathroom."

"Ah. Of course not."

At Nowatari's urging, Sekiguchi moved to the study across the corridor. Inside were two large bookshelves leaning against the walls, a small shelf with a telephone and a fax machine, and a work desk. Atop the desk was a laptop computer that had been shut down and left open. As far as he could see from the books stacked on the shelves and spread around the computer, this room housed more novels and popular titles than it did research material.

On the other side of the closed door, he could hear the muted sound of footsteps as Nowatari went downstairs to the bathroom. It wasn't long before the wife's muffled voice approached. It lingered in the corridor, intertwined with her husband's soft words, and was followed by the sound of a door closing. They must have gone into the bedroom.

Several minutes later, Nowatari returned to the study.

"Sorry to have kept you waiting. Everything's alright now."

"Ah."

What exactly was alright? Sekiguchi stood there for a moment, unable to quite comprehend the situation. But he had already finished what he had come here to do, and he had no particular reason to stay. Nor did he want to disturb Rui after just having finished bathing. Nonetheless, when they stepped out into the corridor, Nowatari led him to the bedroom once more.

Inside, Sekiguchi realized that there was now something contained within the tank. It was made up of black and beige parts, covered throughout in a murky, pale green. He couldn't make out what it was, but he felt an unpleasant sensation rising in his chest. It was a strange feeling, similar to the kind of nervous premonition that comes over you when you find a dark mass on the side of the road and wonder whether or not it might be a dead body.

At that moment, the clump in front of him suddenly turned his way with a faint rustling sound. Then, a pair of eyes stared straight at him.

"Mr. Sekiguchi." The eyes smiled joyfully. "Sorry to bother you when you're so busy. You're a lifesaver."

Every hair on his body stood on end at the familiar sound of the woman's voice. He didn't *want* to understand what he was looking at, but with every passing second, his comprehension grew only more real.

"R–Rui?"

All across her face and body, ripe, green buds seemed to be sprouting from every pore of her skin. Looking carefully, he could even make out small, round leaves peeking out from the part in her hair. The lower half of her body was buried in the soil that Nowatari had just prepared, and she wore a cream-colored blanket draped around her chest. Shocked by this bizarre scene, Sekiguchi realized that he must have looked at her discourteously, as Rui made an awkward face, letting out an airy laugh.

"Just look what I've gotten myself into."

"A-and what exactly is that?" Unable to believe what he was seeing, he could think of nothing else to say.

At that moment, Nowatari stepped back into the room, carrying a green watering can.

"Here you go, Rui," he said quietly, sprinkling a soft shower over her body.

"Ah, soil *is* better. It's much easier absorbing water now."

She exhaled deeply, closed her eyes, and leaned her head against the side of the tank, her expression one of peace and contentment.

"Sorry, I need to rest a moment. Please don't worry about me. Keep going with your work, Tetsuya. The jar of coffee is on the second shelf of the food rack."

"Right."

Following a light nod from Nowatari, Sekiguchi left the couple's bedroom. The two of them made their way downstairs, then sat on the living room sofas in the exact same places that they had occupied during their meeting the day before.

Nowatari breathed a deep sigh. He let his gaze drift for a few seconds and then, looking uncomfortable, rose back to his feet.

"Right. Coffee, wasn't it?"

"Mr. Nowatari? I'll do it."

"No, it's fine. Sit, please."

The coffee was weak and bitter. He must have used the lukewarm water that had been left over in the kettle. Rui no doubt boiled a fresh pot each time. Nonetheless, Sekiguchi forced himself to drink it down before carefully addressing the writer: "Um, have you thought about taking her to a hospital? I'm not sure what kind of specialist you would need to see though . . . A dermatologist, maybe?"

"She doesn't want to. No matter what I say, she won't listen. I thought about calling an ambulance, but she threatened to bite her tongue off if I so much as tried."

"That's . . ."

"We were having a fight. All these minor misunderstandings just piled up . . . and then she did this to get back at me."

Sekiguchi recalled the conversation that he had overheard between the two of them while they were in the bathroom.

Nowatari taught a creative writing course at the local cultural center once a month. Was his wife suspicious of his relationship with one of the women in his class? Sekiguchi had never paid it any particular attention before, but now that he thought about it, the writer *did* have well-defined facial features, the kind that women might indeed find attractive. He was well dressed, with a relaxed sense of style and an approachable self-confidence. Not only that, but he had a well-toned physique for a man in his forties. It wouldn't have been beyond the realm of believability if he *had* entertained one or two extramarital dalliances.

With a grimace, Nowatari crossed his arms and cleared his throat. "Well, it's nothing. This is a problem for us to sort out as a couple. I'll find a way to clear it up and get her to see a doctor."

"I see . . ."

"More importantly, I'm thinking of changing the setting of my next novel. It will probably take me a while to sort it all out, so can we make the deadline a little more flexible?"

"Yes, of course!"

Now that the conversation had turned to business, Sekiguchi hurriedly sat upright and pulled a notepad from his breast pocket.

The theme was to be miscommunication between men and women, with the story revolving around a couple who suddenly found themselves always talking at cross-purposes, Nowatari explained. In that case, there had been a foreign work a short while back that might make for good reference material, Sekiguchi suggested.

After an animated discussion that lasted almost two hours, Sekiguchi finally left the Nowatari residence. It was already late. Normally when he lingered this long, Rui might have prepared a simple meal for him, a bowl of ramen noodles or a plate of okonomiyaki.

But that wouldn't be possible anymore. How would Nowatari, who had always been so dependent on his wife, live from now on? At the office, Sekiguchi often heard about instances of marital trouble, cases where one party or the other came down with a major illness or passed away, where they were caught having an affair, or where there was a pregnancy due to infidelity—but this had to be the first time that he had ever heard of anyone's wife sprouting saplings.

He drove the company car from the vacant lot, returned the cart to the home center, and made his way back to the office. On his way home, he ate a quick dinner at the stand-up soba noodle bar on the station platform, changed trains a few times, and arrived back at his apartment. By then, it was already around ten o'clock. He opened the front door quietly so as not to wake the children, and with the lights turned low, walked into the living room.

At the same time, his wife, Akiko, stepped out from the tatami-floored room after putting their children to sleep. The two of them exchanged silent nods, and he waited for her to slide the door shut before turning the lights up in the living room.

"I'm back."

"Have you eaten dinner? There's some gapao rice left over."

"I had some noodles on the way back."

"Oh."

Stifling a yawn, Akiko sat down in front of the coffee table and pulled some documents from her work bag. Then, after tapping her mechanical pencil against the table, she rubbed her temples and sank deep into thought. She was probably writing out a shift schedule for the store where she worked.

Akiko had originally been employed as an accountant at the headquarters of a global apparel chain. However, soon after returning to the workplace after her second maternity leave, she had found it impossible to strike a balance between her childcare and professional duties. As such, around six months ago, she changed from a regular full-time position to a part-time one with little overtime and started working as an assistant manager at a store closer to home.

Since the transfer meant giving up her career, and given that at the time they had essentially had double incomes, Sekiguchi had suggested that she should instead hire a babysitter to look after the children. However, he could see now that her decision had been for the best. Their schedules hadn't aligned well when they were both working full-time, and it hadn't been unusual for them to spend entire days without seeing each other despite living under the same roof. Now, when he came home, Akiko was almost always there to greet him, and their children could eat their mother's homemade cooking before being tucked off to bed with a lullaby. He felt a sense of domestic comfort, as though a mere roommate had finally become family.

After taking a shower, he gulped down a canful of beer while nodding along as Akiko made a fuss about all the unfinished work that she had brought home.

"I'm working ten times more than that idiot manager, who can't even sort out the part-timers' rosters, and I'm getting paid half as much. It's unbelievable!"

"Well, you can move your shifts around if the kids get sick, so that flexibility is worth half your old salary, right? You can't really complain, given all that luxury."

Akiko wrinkled her brow. Even now, she still ended up in a bad mood whenever they talked about her balancing childcare and work. Sekiguchi threw the empty beer can in the trash and promptly retreated to the tatami-floored room where the children were sleeping.

In the dim blue darkness, two soft, round shapes lay sleeping a short distance apart. The children's room always smelled oily and sugary with a scent of baked sweets. Lying down between the two, he stroked the head of his five-year-old son, who lay dozing curled up on his side, before inserting a finger into the tiny palm of his one-year-old daughter, who was sleeping faceup with her arms spread out. The way that she weakly held on to his finger was nothing short of adorable.

With his workload increasing year after year due to a shortage of personnel at the editorial department, Sekiguchi left for the office at seven o'clock in the morning and didn't usually get home until ten in the evening. He hardly ever had an opportunity to see his children awake except on weekends and holidays. Just looking at their innocent sleeping faces filled his heart with affection and gave him the strength to go back to work the following day. It was thanks to them that he could carefully read over the endless stacks of proofs that landed on his desk, pointing out any errors and issues in the manuscripts of a wide assortment of authors while taking care not to bruise their professional pride or their motivation to produce high-quality literary works. He stared absently at the ceiling, looking back on cases that had required him to coordinate with the sales department on a manuscript, or problems that could only be solved by liaising with various different parties and stakeholders.

Waah, rose a voice beside him. With a wail that sounded almost like a cat sneezing, his daughter crumpled her face and began to wriggle and squirm. She loved to cling to her mother's breast, and she wouldn't stop crying until she was held in her arms. She was adorable when she cried too. Sekiguchi watched on for a brief moment, until Akiko slid open the door and strode in with a scowl.

"Not again . . . Alright, alright. What's wrong?" she said in a soft singsong voice, scooping their daughter from her futon and carrying her back to the living room.

As Sekiguchi let the soft lullabies wash over him, all thought of work faded from his mind, and he drifted off into a dreamless sleep.

IN GENERAL, SEKIGUCHI believed that the problems that arose within families were best resolved by the members of those families themselves. Even if, for example, their child was skipping school, or their wife hospitalized, or their husband suffering from depression, as independent members of society, everyone in the company ought to be able to maintain their sense of composure and carry on with their duties, taking care not to cause any problems or discomfort for those around them.

That was why, as far as he was concerned, the trouble between the Nowatari couple was something for the two of them to solve. He couldn't be blamed for looking on with a certain optimism and indifference, as if watching a house fire on the opposite bank of a river.

To be honest, he tried his best not to think about Rui's unusual situation until Nowatari sent him an early draft of his next work. In all truth, what he had seen was so unsettling that he perhaps hadn't *wanted* to think about it. Just what kind of treatment was there for someone whose body was being consumed by plants? Would those germinated seeds have to be pulled out of her pores one by one with a pair of tweezers? At times, he found his abject sense of curiosity getting the better of him.

The novel draft, around fifty manuscript pages in length, was about a woman who, chewing over her relationship with a man, gulped down a mouthful of plant seeds, only to then have green shoots sprout from every pore of her body.

Deprived of nourishment by the growing saplings, the woman's body grew weaker and more meager by the day, until at last she became one with the damp, black soil. Her apricot-colored lips, still ripe and ample, moved in the shadows of the lustrous, overgrown leaves: *This is how much I loved you.*

The moment that he read that graphic sentence, Sekiguchi rose to his feet, a cold shiver coursing down his spine. He phoned Nowatari to confirm that he was at home, brought the printed manuscript with him to read as he boarded first one train, then the next, and then took a taxi from the nearest station.

"I feel kind of bad, making you come all this way."

Nowatari, whom Sekiguchi hadn't seen in more than a week, had the swollen face of a man who had just woken up. Stifling a yawn, he led the editor through to a living room that was even more disordered than it had been during his last visit.

"I've been all groggy since I sent the manuscript in, and I haven't been able to sleep well. In this state, I don't think I'm going to be able to get my head around your feedback."

"No, it isn't anything too complicated . . . Er, you're modeling this story on your wife, aren't you?"

"Yeah. I've been giving it a bit of thought. What's happening to her is a whole lot more interesting than those other half-baked ideas I had."

"*Interesting* . . . ? She *did* go to a hospital after I saw her last time, right? She *did* get treatment for it?"

"No. She said she doesn't want to."

"Excuse me?"

"She says she's happy like this, that she doesn't want to go back to the way things were. I give up," he said in a sluggish drawl as he scratched his scalp through his disarranged bed hair. "It's no good. I can't keep my eyes open. If you need anything, wake me up in half an hour." He lay down on the sofa and fumbled around for a nearby blanket.

"But Mr. Nowatari, what about Rui?"

"Ah, right. Sekiguchi, if you don't mind hanging around, can you give her a little water? I was so busy writing last night that I forgot all about her. The soil has probably gone dry by now." As he pulled the blanket up to his chin, Nowatari lifted an arm over the back of the sofa and pointed toward the kitchen.

There was a green watering can on the floor.

WHEN ALL WAS said and done, this problem was a matter for the Nowatari couple—or at least it should have been.

Unconsciously grinding his teeth, Sekiguchi filled the watering can and carried it upstairs. He set it down on the floor so as not to spill its contents, nudged open the bedroom door, took it in his arms once again, and entered the dimly lit room.

The couple's bedroom was somewhat humid.

The air flowed softly, as though a large, breathing creature occupied the space.

Sekiguchi's eyes were drawn to an overgrown mass in the corner of the room. He was struck by an ominous feeling, his chest all but choking on what felt like some cloying black ooze. Dozens of thin, straight stems were jutting forth from the wide water tank, almost reaching up to his chest in height. In the narrow space at the base of those plants, a lump of pale flesh lay curled up in a fetal position, legs and arms tucked in under its head.

Both the author's wife, who was willing to go this far, and the author himself, who had surrendered to her will, were clearly insane. Even more so if the cause of the wife's bizarre behavior was her husband's infidelity. What Sekiguchi saw before him was nothing more than the disastrous final stage of an act of adultery—the breakdown of a relationship and a self-destructive desperation.

So why was the woman whom Nowatari had depicted in his latest work so excruciatingly beautiful? She was innocent, foolish, painfully compassionate, yet wounded and bleeding. A raw stench of immorality, almost like the familiar scent of lilies, seemed to waft from each line.

It was *Tears* all over again. Sekiguchi had no doubt that the author's next work would be a masterpiece that peeled back the layers of human karma, the eternal cycle of action and consequence. The first three lines alone were enough to give him that impression.

The manuscript began with the title *Chapter 1*. In other words, the second and third chapters were bound to follow.

If it was ever to be completed, the small hell born in the water tank in front of him would no doubt be a necessary sacrifice.

His mind went blank.

His hands were devoid of feeling as he tilted the watering can. The sleeping faces of his children floated up before his eyes. Their small, maple leaf–shaped palms, the fragrant scent that arose from the whorls of their hair. He wanted nothing more than to cast the watering can aside and return to that peaceful bedroom. Water erupted from the sprinkler at the end of the spout, like raindrops drenching the overgrown leaves and sliding down the long stems.

"Oh, that feels good . . ."

All of a sudden, a woman's voice gushed up from the bottom of the tank. It was a familiar voice, but at the same time, he had never heard Rui sound more cheerful. He was shocked that she could still speak in her condition.

"Mr. Sekiguchi. I'm so sorry Tetsuya made you do this. I'm afraid there really is no helping him when he gets dug into his work."

He had to respond. Whatever her physical state, this woman—*was* she still a woman? a clump of earth? a person? a nursery bed?—was the wife of an important business partner and the source of that man's inspiration. He had to treat her with respect.

He understood that, and yet his tongue refused to move. He couldn't help but feel that if he was to say something, anything, he would become complicit in Nowatari's actions. This horrifying situation, and the literary work based on it, were ultimately Nowatari's sin. Sekiguchi was just supposed to receive his breathtaking manuscript and deliver it to the world. The publishing house was merely a conduit linking supply and demand. His job was no more than that, he repeated to himself over and over.

"I'm usually the one to serve you tea whenever you have a meeting with Tetsuya, but today it looks like it's the other way around," the overgrown leaves swayed in a whisper. They were smiling.

Sekiguchi felt a sudden welling up of hatred for this insane couple, who seemed to lack even the slightest comprehension of the terror of their situation. His hands trembling, he finished emptying the watering can into the tank and left the bedroom without uttering so much as a word.

He wasn't able to bring himself to go straight home. After stepping off the train at the downtown station where he normally changed lines, he bought a woman at the entertainment district for the first time in what felt like ages. He hadn't come to the pink salon since he had first joined the company, when a senior colleague had taken him out on the town. The girl looked to be over thirty yet claimed to be only twenty-one years old. Her large cleavage was covered in red acne, but her touch was gentle. After the act was over, she hugged him until his time was up, and so he returned home, his mood somewhat lightened.

"You're late."

Akiko had brought her work home again today, spreading it out before her on the coffee table. She was clearly exhausted, flipping through a thick file of what looked like product descriptions and taking notes on a ground plan of the sales floor while sipping at a can of beer. Overcome by guilt, Sekiguchi couldn't look her in the eyes. He explained that he was having some trouble with a book that he was working on.

Akiko's face clouded over. "Don't overdo it, okay? Are you letting those bigwigs push you around again?"

"No, it isn't like that. It's just . . ."

"It's just," he muttered again, but his mouth grew heavy before he could finish his train of thought. He was stricken by temptation bordering on vertigo, to tell her, to confess to his longtime companion what he had encountered today, what he had been forced to do, and to come clean. He wanted to wash his hands of it all, and for her to comfort him, telling him that everything would be okay.

Sekiguchi clenched his mouth shut.

There was no way that he would be able to say all that to her.

Was he going to stand by and do nothing while another man's wife lay dying, all for the sake of one story? Was he going to be complicit in that act of murder? Only someone who had fallen into the same situation as he had would be able to understand the context, to sympathize with his predicament. Akiko would look on him with fear and trepidation, as though he had become a loathsome insect.

"We're just having a little disagreement, that's all. We'll sort it out in a few days."

"Well, if you're sure . . ."

"I'm going to take a bath."

A scent, of the woman from the pink salon mixed with the smell of alcohol, lingered at the tip of his nose. She probably rubbed her breasts down with a wet wipe after each customer. Only after he had washed himself with his usual body soap and familiar-smelling shampoo was he finally able to relax his shoulders.

When he returned to the living room, Akiko was holding his phone.

"You got a notification. I thought it might have been someone from work, but it was just an app up-date. Go charge it. The battery's about to run out, you know?" Akiko said with exasperation as she handed it back to him.

TEN DAYS LATER, Sekiguchi received the second chapter from Nowatari. The quiet dialogue between a woman who was becoming increasingly removed from her sense of humanity and the unremarkable, commonplace man who had once loved her was heartbreaking.

The editorial department was so impressed that they decided to plan immediately for a paperback sales strategy and release date, even before putting the work through the usual process of magazine serialization.

"Mr. Nowatari has missed out on the major prizes a few times now, but he might finally have a real chance with this one."

"He seems to have taken a new turn with the way he's writing the female character. He's normally careful to maintain their beauty until the end of the story, but this time, he's bringing her to ruin from the very beginning."

"Excellent work, Sekiguchi. How on earth did you get him to write this?"

The entire editorial department was in a state of excitement at the prospect of this impending success. Everyone stopped by his desk to give him a friendly compliment, to tell him how great the manuscript was, that Nowatari wasn't just a one-hit wonder. Each time, Sekiguchi felt like he was swallowing down a stone. He hadn't done anything wrong, he told himself. He was simply doing his job.

Nonetheless, he carefully observed the reaction of the chief editor, Tanahashi, as he perused the work. He had no intention of whining that he didn't want to be involved in the manuscript anymore. But if he could, if he could have said something, how would he phrase it? Could he say that Nowatari's wife was in trouble, and yet in spite of that, the author just kept pouring himself into the manuscript, and . . . and what? What exactly had he gotten himself caught up in?

During the morning meeting, the weak, flickering flame of his hesitation dissipated the moment that Tanahashi raised his eyebrows as his gaze coursed down the printout.

"I wonder . . . It almost feels like Nowatari is maturing as a writer, but it doesn't seem all that different from the other things he's given us up till now."

Sekiguchi felt a swell of anger rising up inside him, enough to make his chest hurt.

Did Tanahashi have any idea what he had had to

go through, how far he had been forced to dirty his hands for the sake of this manuscript?

He took a deep breath, exhaled slowly, and responded in a calm voice: "Please wait for the final section. I'm sure it will be Mr. Nowatari's masterpiece."

"There's no denying that it's interesting. The physical decay of the body certainly has a strong impact. It easily meets our standard for publication. It's just . . . well, maybe if he had a little more self-doubt, if he could push himself to experience a little more suffering or anguish, there might be more to it . . . Hmm. Well, we can hardly ask him to make major changes to it now. Let's see how he wraps it up."

"Yes. Thank you."

After the meeting, Sekiguchi took the train again to the Nowatari residence. He found the author, exhausted from writing, slumped back into the sofa, practically one with the furniture.

"Good news!" he announced with excitement. "Let's keep it up!"

"Yeah, I'm in the flow of it now. I think it's going to be really good this time." There were dark circles under Nowatari's eyes, but that didn't stop him from flashing Sekiguchi an innocent grin. "Sorry about this, but I've been too tired this morning to look after Rui. Can you give her some water?"

There was no turning back now. Sekiguchi forced

his stiffened lips into a faint smile and gave the author a short nod.

The watering can, filled to the top, was just as heavy as he remembered it.

When he opened the door, he saw that the plants in the water tank were already stretching all the way up to the ceiling. Many of those stems, which had been as thick as spears of asparagus the last time that he had seen them, were now the width of beer cans, their warped shapes overflowing from the tank. The cramped roots and the thick swell of their trunks reminded him of a head of broccoli. The seeds must have spilled over the edge of the tank, as grass had begun to sprout from the carpet surrounding it. A full third of the room had been invaded by the greenery.

Was it possible for trees to grow so quickly by feeding off the life of a person?

A chill ran down his spine as he poured the water into the narrow gaps between the thick stalks, so tightly packed that they might force the tank to rupture at any moment.

"Ah, Mr. Sekiguchi."

A woman's voice, as cheerful as ever, squeezed his heart.

So she was still alive . . .

"Summer is just around the corner, isn't it? Can

you smell chlorine? They must be disinfecting the pool at the elementary school behind the house."

How he wanted to get this over with as quickly as possible . . . He tilted the watering can steeper.

"I suppose there will be a nice breeze outside, light and warm. It must be lovely. The beginning of summer is my favorite time of year. I wish I could go outside. That man is so thoughtless, leaving all the windows closed like this. I feel like I'm suffocating."

What on earth was this woman—woman? being?—saying? Hadn't she let go of her human body of her own accord, and with it the ability to go wherever she wanted, to do whatever she pleased? Sekiguchi gazed over the contents of the tank, over the mass of intricately intertwined roots. Was she living inside all that? Was she watching him from in there, her eyes following him from behind some dark crevice?

Sekiguchi suddenly realized that he no longer recognized Rui as a human being. She had become some otherworldly entity beyond his abilities of comprehension. Even if it was possible to find a slither of beauty in someone who clothed themselves in vegetation in some kind of artistic endeavor, once they deviated too far from base humanity, the only response could be one of unbearable revulsion. Entities that were like people but not, that occupied the ambiguous space between human and *thing*, were nothing short of terrifying. He checked to make sure that the watering can was empty before hurriedly retreating from the bedroom.

After having visited the pink salon the first time, the feeling of relief that he had taken from it developed into a habit, and he found himself stopping by again on his way home. Nonetheless, the woman assigned to him failed to strike his fancy, and when he made his way back to his apartment, he only felt more tired.

The second that he opened the front door, he knew that something was amiss. The room was dark. The living room lights weren't dimmed like when the children were put to bed—they were completely off. He couldn't remember the last time he had come home to total darkness.

He reached around for the light switch and turned it on. On the coffee table where Akiko usually worked was a sheet of A4 paper crammed with a disquieting block of handwritten text:

I don't know why we're living together anymore if you don't love me I wish you would say so I'm taking the kids why don't you hold them when they cry you probably don't care about them anyway do you you act like I'm your mother I'd sooner get a divorce and go back to my parents I can't keep living like this always passing each other by all the time living separate lives, and so on.

The characters were at first neat and tidy, but as

the rows progressed, the writing descended into a tangled mess of intertwined curves and lines. The letter was so out of the blue that no matter how many times he read it, he simply couldn't wrap his head around it. Had he come home to the wrong house? If he were to retrace his steps, maybe turn down a different street or get off the train a station earlier, he was sure that he would find everything just the way that it had been before. Akiko would be there murmuring to herself as she worked at the coffee table, his adorable children would be sound asleep in their bedroom, and the fridge would be filled with cans of ice-cold beer. His real home, *his* home, was out there somewhere, waiting for him.

Was this, he wondered, how Nowatari had felt when Rui first germinated?

IT WAS THE height of summer when Nowatari submitted the third and final chapter. Without waiting for the author to prompt him, Sekiguchi made his way with the heavy watering can upstairs and into the couple's bedroom, now almost entirely overgrown with plants.

Even if he wanted to water it, he wasn't even sure where the tank was anymore. The floor was covered in knee-high bushes, and there were other trees growing all throughout the room as well, the foliage so thick that he couldn't even see the wall on the far side. He was amazed that the floor hadn't given way under all that weight.

Faced with no other choice, he sprinkled the water in the area where he vaguely remembered the tank being. He could locate neither the bed nor the bookshelves and was left with only a weak sense of his position inside the room.

He was halfway through pouring the water, and still the forest remained silent. There was no hint of Rui's lively voice.

Was she finally dead?

With her gaze gone, Sekiguchi was at last able to calmly take in the forest. In his confusion and fear over what Rui had become, he must have looked at it without properly seeing anything on his last few visits here. Except for the fact that it was indoors, the dimly lit forest was much like any other wooded area on the outskirts of town. The trees and grasses all looked familiar, and there was no hint of any threat or disturbance.

He felt guilty now over his prior terror. The last time that he had seen Rui, hadn't she been more like someone in the final stages of a terminal illness than the living monster that he had taken her for? She hadn't ended up that way by choice. It was all because of Nowatari. That being the case, shouldn't he at least have offered her some small gesture, to nod along in pleasant small talk, to offer to listen to her regrets to help alleviate any sense of lingering resentment?

As he strained his eyes, he found that nuts and seeds of all shapes and sizes had spilled out onto the carpet, covered with undergrowth.

I wish I could go outside, her voice echoed back to him. Sekiguchi crouched down, gathering the nuts and seeds by his feet and stuffing them into his suit pocket. Nowatari's sin-wracked novel was now complete. From here on out, Sekiguchi would be kept busy promoting it. He probably wouldn't have cause to visit this room again for a while.

He spotted a thin beam of light in a corner of the forest. Suspicious, he forced his way through the bushes, ducking under the branches as he made his way toward it. The room was only around ten tatami mats in size, so he should have bumped straight into the wall, but perhaps because he was unable to properly make out his surroundings, it seemed to have acquired a greater sense of depth.

The source of light was the bedroom window. It was mostly covered by a shroud of leaves and vines, but it was still leaking thin pillars of illumination from all four sides. Standing on his tiptoes so as not to crush the plants underfoot, he groped for the crescent lock and pushed it open in a single motion.

A hot, humid breeze swept through the overgrown

room. The air smelled of chlorine, the chirring of ci-
cadas assaulted his ears, and a brilliant midsummer
sky bore down on him from above. It made him
think of Akiko. How was she spending this summer
with the children? No matter how many times he
tried to contact her, he had received no response.
There was nothing to suggest that she meant to come
back to him.

Where had she and the children disappeared to?

The surrounding leaves trembled all at once. The
forest was laughing.

2

KINARI YUKO WAS SITTING IN THE CAFÉ ON the top floor of the cultural school building when she heard the rumor—Nowatari Tetsuya's wife had apparently run away from home.

Her hand froze in midair, the half-melted spoonful of watermelon ice cream falling to the table with a soft plop. As she watched the ice cream slowly melt away, she listened to the conversation taking place behind her. Yatabe Keiko and her friend Oshima Kaori, both of whom were attending the same creative writing course as her, were getting all worked up as they engaged in small talk. The two of them were housewives whose children had left the nest, and they both spent their free time writing quiet romances in which modest men and women would fall in love against one beautiful backdrop or another.

"It's true. We live in the same neighborhood. I used to bump into his wife all the time at the convenience store and the local supermarket, but there's been no sign of her for three months now. Their house is in bad shape too. The second floor is completely overgrown with houseplants. Really, they're spilling out all over the place."

"Oh? That's . . . surprising. Mr. Nowatari doesn't seem like the kind of person to get into that sort of trouble."

"People like that, those herbivore-types, you would be surprised to know how many problems they really have. You know, they could be gambling addicts, or the kind to mess around with young women."

The watermelon ice cream that had fallen to the table quickly melted into a bright-red puddle. Even if it was still composed of the same ingredients as before, now that it had melted, it had become a disgusting, sloppy stain. Kinari wiped it up with a paper napkin and ate the rest of the ice cream in silence, before stopping the waitress to order another cup of coffee. The hot, freshly brewed liquid soaked into her numbed tongue.

EACH TIME THAT she wondered how the situation might have come to this, Kinari found herself thinking back to a certain childhood memory, a day when she had gone up to the mountains to find the source of a local river.

The trip had been organized specifically for children, run by the neighborhood association or some such group. Led by the young owner of a local soba noodle restaurant, Kinari, together with close to a dozen other children, each equipped with hats and backpacks and dressed in long sleeves and trousers, climbed the mountain path that followed the course of the river.

It's really lame, one of the other children had said to her earlier. And what they found was indeed pitiful. The two-hour journey to the headwaters deep in the mountains uncovered only the unsatisfying sight of water trickling from the seams of rocks protruding from a cliff edge. They each took turns putting their faces to the cliffside to take a few sips, but it was just normal water, cool to the touch.

Nonetheless, that disappointing discovery left a strong impression on her.

She wondered whether those lonely droplets spilling slowly down the cliff edge had any idea that they would one day combine into a great river.

KINARI'S REASON FOR signing up to the creative writing course was simple—a coupon for a free trial course of her choice at the cultural school had appeared one day in her mailbox.

She remembered having seen the name Nowatari Tetsuya several times before on the shelves in the library. It looked like this could be a chance for her to have a professional author evaluate her writing.

Now that her children had entered elementary school, things were finally beginning to settle down at home, and she thought that it would be nice if she could write a letter to an old friend of hers who lived far away. It was in this lighthearted frame of mind that she filled out the application form and faxed it to the cultural school. Now that she thought about it, she might have confused a writing course with a *creative* writing course.

She found, when Nowatari Tetsuya entered the classroom, that his most striking characteristics were his silver-rimmed glasses and his calm demeanor. He was the kind of man with whom she would have felt comfortable speaking at a parent-teacher conference. His general aura wasn't at all that of an eminent teacher or a cultural champion.

However, it had been a long time since she had met a man like him, older than herself, with a full head of hair, albeit graying, no paunch to his stomach, and seemingly not of ill-humored disposition. She felt as though she had stumbled upon something wonderful, like a cloudless, scarlet dusk, or a puddle of water that glistened like a perfect mirror. Nowatari's mustard-colored shirt suited his relaxed profile.

Her first task was to write a short story on a single four hundred–character sheet of manuscript paper, basing it on a photograph of a middle-aged couple, a man and a woman cuddling under the branches of a tree. She hadn't written anything within a fixed time limit since her student days, and so she wrote and erased, wrote and erased, until she was thoroughly exhausted. Each time, she couldn't proceed any further than a couple of lines, all of them variations on the same general theme—*I love him*. Her paper, when she submitted it, was almost entirely blank. Glancing around the room out of the corner of her vision, she saw that most of the other students were in a similar situation as her. They were called to Nowatari's seat in turn to await his critique.

Nowatari looked down at her manuscript paper, badly wrinkled from too many edits, and called out her name, as if practicing how it felt rolling off the tongue.

"Kinari Yuko. What a beautiful name. I wish I could use it in a novel."

"You *can* use it. Please."

"Do you mean it?"

"Please, go ahead."

Apparently, her parents had found the sunset scenery of the lake outside their honeymoon hotel room especially beautiful, and so had named her Yuko—written with the characters for *evening* and *lake*. Kinari herself didn't like that name at all, as it had been given for such a simple and selfish reason.

That night, as she cleaned up after dinner, she felt a little dizzy. The blank columns on the manuscript

paper appeared before her eyes. It seemed like ages
since anyone had asked her to think so hard in such a
short span of time, and her brain was still somewhat
feverish.

Learning was tiring. But, she thought, it was nice
to try something new every once in a while.

ONE DAY, AROUND three months into the course,
Kinari offered to share with Nowatari some loquat
jellies that she had received as a midyear gift, and
he invited her in turn to enjoy a cup of hojicha tea
with him.

She stayed behind after class, waiting for the other
students to file out of the room before they sat down
across from each other and shared the jelly cups between them. She couldn't help but feel a sense of im-
propriety at the situation—a middle-aged man and
woman, teacher and student at that, taking an infor-
mal break like this—but Nowatari didn't seem at all
bothered.

It wasn't much different from those times prior
to her getting married when she had shared tea and
small talk with a member of the opposite sex, certainly nothing to be too concerned over, she thought.
She had been kept so busy after the birth of her first
child that the only people whom she had met face-
to-face in what felt like years were other mothers and

friends of her husband. Perhaps she was being overly sensitive? Yes, that must have been it. So she told herself as she quietly nibbled away at the loquat jelly.

Nowatari sipped at his tea, paused to catch his breath for a second, and addressed her, his expression serious: "Truth be told, for such a beautiful name as yours, I was rather surprised by how lonely it is."

"Oh?"

She was taken aback. How could he describe someone's name as lonely? People often complimented her name, told her that it was beautiful or had a certain atmosphere about it, but never before had someone so openly disparaged it.

"I tried to give it to a character I'm writing, but it didn't really work. The image of a lake at dusk was just too strong."

"Is a sunset lake really that lonely?"

"Yes, very. All that water shimmering in the setting sun, those gradations from light orange all the way to bluish purple, you know? It makes you wonder what kind of person a character would have to be to embody that kind of scene."

Unsure how to respond to this display of pathos, Kinari let out a small chuckle, like a bubble floating up to the surface. She wondered whether all novelists were like this, asking people what sort of lives they led as though it were a matter of course. It was just so strange.

"I mean, I'm just a normal person. Maybe a little boring."

"Hmm . . . I'd like to speak with you more, Yuko. So I can work out how to use your name better in a future work." Nowatari rested his chin on his hands as he peered toward her.

The moment that she caught sight of a mischievous glint in his eyes, a drop of warmth dripped down, moistening her heart.

THE CREATIVE WRITING course was held once a month on a Saturday afternoon. Before long, Kinari started meeting with Nowatari before or after class to chat over a simple lunch, a plate of curry or a bowl of soba noodles.

"You can drop the *Mr.* There's no need to address me so formally outside of class," Nowatari said to her as he spooned a large helping of grated radish into a cup of dipping sauce on their first such meeting.

"But even outside of class, you're still a novelist . . . Isn't it normal to address novelists that way?"

"You only need to do that for great novelists."

"But aren't you a great novelist . . . Nowatari?"

"Not at all. I still haven't written a truly great novel, the kind that really surprises people."

It was disconcerting to think that a man with his name on so many books in the library could think

of himself so modestly. After adding the grated radish, Nowatari threw in a helping of wasabi paste and
sliced green onion, and for his first bite, sampled not
his soba noodles but the shrimp tempura that he had
ordered as a side dish. Perhaps he wasn't particularly
fond of the taste of soba noodles? Only after polish-
ing off the entire shrimp, tail and all, did he dip the
noodles into the oily sauce.

Kinari had always entertained a mental image
of novelists as being delicate gourmets, but that apparently wasn't the case. Feeling like she was in the
presence of an everyday person not too unlike herself, she silently slurped her own bowlful of wakame
soba noodles. Her husband was so particular about
food that he would have first sampled the noodles by
themselves, and only then would he have tried dipping them in the sauce. Nor would he have dissolved
the wasabi paste in it—as far as he was concerned,
that was for placing on the noodles directly.

She wondered when she had last eaten alone with
a man other than her husband. But this was nothing
more than a simple social gathering between teacher
and student. She was being interviewed by a novelist,
she as a housewife, he as a teacher, and that was all
that there was to it.

But was it really?

Finding herself growing more confused by the
second, she ended up blurting out: "There are some

things I wanted to tell you that you might be able to use in your novel!" And so she began to relate a wide range of strange occurrences that she remembered from her student days or her time as an office worker. There was this person or that one, a ghost story here and there. Nowatari nodded along, but he didn't seem to be listening particularly carefully.

Perhaps her stories weren't all that interesting? She glanced uncertainly at his face, only to find him watching her with a grin.

"What's so funny?" she demanded, thinking that he was toying with her.

Nowatari's smile deepened. "Ah. I was just thinking how worried you look, how attentive you are. How cute."

"What are you saying . . . ?"

"But why are you so fidgety? We're just here to have a bite to eat and a casual chat. That's all."

Even if that *was* all that there was to it, she was who she was. She was always fretting over whether others enjoyed being with her, whether they weren't uncomfortable around her. She was always doing her best to play up to them, to keep them in a good mood.

"Yes," Kinari stammered in explanation.

Nowatari's eyes opened wide. "Why?" he asked once more.

Faced with such a direct question, she found

herself lost for words yet again. Why? Why *did* she always end up trying to ingratiate herself with people?

Nowatari sat watching her, propping his chin on
his hands.

Five seconds passed, then ten, before she gave up
on looking for an answer and mouthed: "How are
you able to see so much?"

"Because I'm staring into a lake."

"Huh?"

"It's a wide, fathomless lake, with beautiful colors scintillating over the surface of the water. I don't
think you realize just how splendid you are, Yuko."
Nowatari chuckled, the corners of his eyes wrinkling
wonderfully.

The droplets started falling all over again, pitter-
patter, without end.

Like an approaching evening shower, those warm
droplets gradually increased in intensity, until before
she knew it, they had become an irresistible down-
pour that drenched her entire body.

One after another, they dripped down, pooled,
and with a great swell, overflowed into a single
torrent.

AS AUTUMN DEEPENED, the two of them found
themselves in a hotel room.

By that time, their schedules permitting, they

had begun to meet even on days when they had no class. It was always Nowatari who called her. They had shared numerous meals as they got to know each other, and with all but exquisite timing, just when Kinari had begun to imagine him naked, he invited her to come with him.

"I've never been to a love hotel before," she murmured, glancing around the room.

Nowatari let out a startled sound. "Oh? You've led a very upstanding life, Yuko."

"Really?"

She couldn't help but wonder. It was true that she had married her husband, whom she had met as her superior at her very first job after graduating from college, and had retired at the time of her first pregnancy. She didn't have much experience with romance, and her husband was the first man with whom she had ever slept. Perhaps it was fair enough to say that she had lived an upstanding life.

But would a truly upstanding woman engage in an extramarital affair like this?

Yes, Kinari was well aware that this would be adultery. It was a shameless, immoral, filthy, unforgivable act.

She had been expecting something dark and mysterious, but on this noontime weekday, the love hotel was as bright and well lit as the amusement park that she had frequented as a child. She laughed over and over again as she laid eyes on each of the ridiculous and vulgar facilities, from the TV that played adult videos at the touch of a button to the shallow jacuzzi bath to the toilet with no lock on the door. Kissing, hugging, and having sex with someone with whom she had just fallen in love was so exciting that it made even the tips of her fingers tingle.

The two of them made up all sorts of silly games.

For example, Nowatari pretended to be a poor medical student, she a foreign woman who had just escaped from a wicked slave trafficker.

First, Kinari put a rental yukata over her naked skin, stepped out into the corridor of the love hotel, and knocked at the door as she called out in stilted Japanese: "Help me! Help me!" "Who are you, this late at night?" Nowatari replied in false solemnity as he opened the door. She threw herself into his arms, weeping. For the next thirty minutes, she forgot her name, her appearance, her age, and the fact that she was a wife and mother, and she felt that she was allowed to exist only by repeating the embarrassing anatomical words that Nowatari, dressed as a medical student, taught her between their gasps and heavy breathing. It was all so much silly, nonsensical, tear-jerking fun.

Many of the sex situations that Nowatari proposed featured women with unusual quirks. Women who couldn't walk, women who couldn't speak, women who had been spirited off somewhere far away, frigid

women, amorous women. Kinari enjoyed playing
the part of those lovely, wanton women who were
so unlike herself, yet it always struck her as a little
strange.

"Why can't I just be a normal woman? A housewife, or an office worker?"

"Well, other men's wives have always been the
subject of romances, even in antiquity."

She could tell just from his way of speaking that
he wasn't particularly attracted to that notion of *other
men's wives*.

"You know what they say: if you want to win a
man over, you have to catch him off guard. People's
weaknesses are what make others fall in love with
them. You know, this person is weak in such and
such a regard, so I have to protect them. That's why
women with strong quirks and easily recognizable
flaws are easier to fall in love with."

Kinari had never been attracted to a man's weaknesses before. She had always liked them for their
positive qualities, like how easy they were to speak
with or their levelheadedness.

But there was one thing that did come to mind.

Kinari's choice of preferred college had been decided by something that her father had said: "She
doesn't have the grades to make it at a national university, so she's better off going to a down-to-earth

women's college rather than aiming too high and missing the mark."

Her mother was in agreement: "Yes, it would be safer for her to go to a regular school."

And so, of the several institutions within easy commuting distance of her parents' home, she selected a private Christian women's college as her first choice.

The following spring, she passed the entrance exams without a hitch and embarked on college life. Nonetheless, whenever she mentioned the name of her school, she was always left bewildered by the reactions that she received in broader society, at her intercollegiate English-language circle, or at the cram school where she worked part-time. *Well aren't we a well-bred young lady!* they might say, always looking at her with the same judgmental eyes. It seemed that the combination of *Christian* and *women's college* gave that sort of impression. She felt ill at ease, even though nothing about her or her family situation had changed from her high school days.

When she went to a drinking party, those reactions became only more remarkable.

"Is your family strict?"

"I bet you've never had a boyfriend, right?"

"Oh, so you vote? I wouldn't have guessed it."

The kind of young lady that the boys around her described as quiet, unaccustomed to men, and attentive and thoughtful when it came to things like cooking and serving food, but had little aptitude for lewd banter and less still for politics or economics, always flashing people a faint, shy smile.

It was easy to be a *young lady* once you got used to it. And surprisingly, boys liked that persona. During her four years of college, more than a dozen men expressed their fondness for her, and she even fell in love with two of them, albeit briefly. She enjoyed going to the movies, shopping, and having fun over unfamiliar drinks. But she had no idea what to talk about when she was alone with them. No idea at all. A stifling silence would ensue, and neither relationship lasted for more than three months before they parted ways. Still, most boys were kind to her.

When she stopped to think about it, what her father meant by the term *down-to-earth* and the *young lady* that those boys envisioned were probably the same thing. A woman ignorant of the world, ignorant of men, had an easily recognizable, even lovable weakness. *Become a woman whom men can love.* Her father had simply been encouraging her to live the way that he thought most advantageous for a member of her sex.

When she graduated college, joined her company, and got engaged to her husband, the most attractive man in the office, her now-mother-in-law praised her as a simple, lovely young lady. Kinari's mother demurred, humbly describing her rather as an unworldly daughter whose only redeeming feature was her docile nature, but it was clear that she was secretly proud of her.

Kinari's parents-in-law welcomed her as just such a down-to-earth, unworldly young lady. So long as it was within walking distance of the family home, her father-in-law offered to pay a lump-sum down payment on an apartment for the two of them. Now that she was married, she had a wealth of topics to talk about with her husband—the children, their everyday living, their parents, life events. She didn't have to worry about engaging him in conversation, and if she had nothing to discuss, she could choose to remain silent. Only a lover would find silence awkward.

Her everyday living was free from want or hardship.

"What are you thinking?" Nowatari pressed his forehead against her own.

She told him that she had been thinking about her home, the apartment where she lived, and then added that her mother-in-law would bring them healthy, preprepared Tupperware-sealed dishes three times a week, that she helped take the children to and from cram school, and that they were a close-knit and happy family.

"A close-knit and happy family," Nowatari repeated with amusement. "Is that really you speaking,
Yuko?"

"What do you mean?"

"I saw you. In the café on the top floor of the cultural school building. You were repeating something
I said to you while we were alone, verbatim. *Writing
about someone's interiority is literature—writing about how
that person interacts with the outside world is entertainment.*
And then you started telling people which of the two
they were better suited for, literature or entertainment, like a fortune-teller."

"Ah . . ."

Her cheeks began to burn. It was a bad habit of
hers, repeating the opinions of people around her
like they were her own. She hadn't meant to offend.
She had just thought that it would be a clever thing
to say, and it had slipped out.

"I'm sorry . . ."

"There's no need to apologize. It was refreshing
to watch someone so innocent." Nowatari rubbed
his cheek against hers, like a cat in greeting. "I'm
thinking of writing a novel, with you as a model for
the main character."

"Oh. Please. My name, you mean?"

"Well, if I use your name, people will know it's
based on you. I don't want anyone to track down my
sweet Yuko. So no. But your personality . . . How

about this? The protagonist will still be called *Yuko*, but the name will be written with the characters for *cotton* and *child*. It has a simple, pretty ring to it. It suits you."

Kinari rolled the new name across her tongue. *Yuko—cotton child*. The scent of linen water grazed the tip of her nose. It was a name that evoked a strong sensuality rising up from the deepest purity, a name replete with chastity and innocence.

"Call me *Yuko*. Not *evening lake—cotton child*."

"*Yuko*."

"Mmm . . ."

With a rush of pleasure, Kinari wrapped her arms around Nowatari's bare back and whispered: "Let's do it." Hers was a hot, sultry voice, one that she had never heard before.

"MOM, ARE YOU upset?" her second-grade son asked.

Snapping back to her senses, she concentrated her strength in her throat and made her best mommy voice: "No. Everything's fine. But . . . *Coochie-coochie-coo!*"

"Ahahahahaha! Stop it!"

Her younger son flapped his arms like a cabbage butterfly as he escaped back to the living room. Then he threw himself down on the carpet next to his elder brother, busy playing on his portable video game

console, and lay sprawled staring across at the small
screen.

That was a close call, Kinari thought, letting out
an unintended sigh. Her mind had wandered as she
peeled a taro, and she must have let her guard down.
Her younger son had come to ask her whether he
could visit a friend on Sunday, and she had responded
with a strangely indifferent "Do whatever you want."
If she had been her usual self, she would have no
doubt tried to extract as many details from him as
she could—which friend, what time, whether there
would be anyone else going too.

Just two hours ago, *Yuko—cotton child*—had been
her whole identity. That presence still lingered on
her flesh.

Merely thinking back on it was enough to make
her lower body throb so hard that she thought that
she might collapse.

She would be unconcerned in disposition, her
speech and movements so languid, but when the
time came to press her skin against the man's, she
would frolic like a child playing in water, and afterward, would gently cradle his head against her naked
breast.

Nowatari too seemed overjoyed by her dissocia-
tive performance as *Yuko*. The sex lasted longer and
longer as he caressed her entire body with his delicate fingers, as he embraced her, overcome with raw

emotion. He became somehow childish. Despite his initial hesitancy, he began to resemble the arrogant and vulnerable protagonists who frequently appeared in his novels.

But when Nowatari became infatuated with *Yuko*, Kinari felt as though she could finally find peace of mind by his side, that this was the only appropriate way for her to behave. She could only let her guard down with someone if she was certain that they too were happy being with her. She didn't know why, but she had been that way ever since she was a child.

"Our inner natures have intersected so perfectly. Could there be any greater happiness?" Nowatari said profoundly.

Ding-dong, sounded the doorbell out of nowhere.

For a brief moment, she had trouble breathing. A visitor at this time of day, with no prior notice? She would have to cook extra for dinner. She wanted to get the children into the habit of going to bed early, but at this rate, they would end up staying up late again. Was it *her*, bringing yet more sweets? They hadn't even eaten dinner yet. She closed her eyes and imagined using a pair of kitchen scissors to cut away all the unruly images that came to mind.

Her mother-in-law was simply a kindhearted woman who liked to play with her grandchildren. She meant no offense, so it was only natural that Ki-nari thank her with a warm smile, she repeated to herself three times over, like a magician reciting an incantation. Then, in the blink of an eye, she found that she could greet her kind mother-in-law with an unclouded mind. After all, the older woman had warmly welcomed her clumsy daughter-in-law into her family, even if she hadn't known how to properly clean or cook, even if, at the time, she truly hadn't known how to do anything at all to look after a family. It was her mother-in-law who had painstakingly taught her the basics, from how to make soup stock to the proper way to sweep with a broom. Because, she had told her, those were the sorts of things that revealed a person's true nature.

As expected, when Kinari opened the front door, she was greeted by her good-humored mother-in-law, who lived no more than five minutes away by foot, holding a large cloth-covered tray in her hands.

"Good evening, Yuko. Would you look at this? See how perfectly these adzuki and pumpkin puddings have come out! I saw them on the three o'clock cooking show. They're supposed to be so healthy. Perfect for Tomo and Shu, don't you think?"

"Th-thank you. We can have them after dinner then . . ."

"Oh no, they're supposed to be eaten warm. They're best fresh. Tomo! Shu! I've brought pudding!"

Her mother-in-law was a good person, Kinari repeated to herself.

Surrounded by her cheering grandchildren, her mother-in-law smiled happily. Yes, she might visit three times a week, but still she showered her grandchildren with extra-special affection. That being the case, Kinari could afford to be flexible with the rules of the house whenever she called. That was the sort of daughter-in-law who made for a kind and caring mother. She slowly lost sight of what was irritating her. After all, her mother-in-law and her children looked so joyful.

Her mother-in-law's homemade puddings were monotonous in flavor. Nonetheless, the children, whose daily intake of sweets had dropped considerably ever since Kinari had decided to limit the amount of sugar that they consumed, were ecstatic, and they devoured two each.

The ginger-fried pork and komatsuna namul that she set on the table went largely untouched. She had prepared extra for her mother-in-law just in case, but the older woman left early to ready her husband's evening drink. Kinari rushed the children into the bath and put them to bed an hour later than usual.

Finally able to relax, she switched on the TV and began to nibble away at the untouched food.

Less than ten minutes after she had sat down at the dining table, the front door opened as her husband arrived home.

"Welcome back."

"Yeah."

She rose to her feet to dish out his dinner and to prepare a serving of pickles and a glass of beer. Her husband, exhausted, sat down at his place at the table, loosened his tie, and turned his gaze to the TV.

The news was on.

Uh-oh. She had switched over to it, without thinking, to check the weather, but a politics segment started playing at the most inopportune moment, and his brow creased in a frown.

"Nothing but idiots on TV these days. See him? He might have a smooth tongue and a friendly face, but he comes from a yakuza family, and he's not even Japanese. People like him are always trying to rip us normal hardworking folk off. Hey, are you listening? Sit down."

"Yes. Of course."

Holding a glass of beer in one hand, Kinari nodded along to the incessant abuse, all but saying that she didn't really understand these complicated topics, but that if her husband thought so, then it had to be true.

He was tired. He was probably taking out his pent-up frustration from his relentless work schedule on the people on the other side of the TV. Gathering personal information online on the politicians, celebrities, and athletes whom he so disliked and raining insults on them while he watched TV was practically his daily pastime. He earned a steady monthly income, drank modestly, and didn't gamble. On his days off, he took his sons out to play.

He wasn't a bad person. She just wished that they could talk about something else every now and then. Her husband might have had a strong sense of justice and a clarity that could penetrate the serious issues to which most Japanese closed their eyes, but he would probably never realize just how painful it was to have to listen to someone else's trivial grouching at the end of an exhausting day.

Leaving her husband to watch the TV in anger, she casually slipped out from the room and decided to try to get some rest. She made her way to their bedroom and laid out a pair of futons on the tatami-lined floor. The children had been sleeping in a bunk bed in their own room since her younger son started elementary school.

She stared up at the dark ceiling, letting out an exhale. As she tried to nod off to sleep, she found herself thinking about *Yuko*. The sickly sweet memories of her time with Nowatari relieved the tension in her head and lulled her to drowsiness. It was easier being *Yuko*. It was easier than facing the people around her—her children, her mother-in-law, her husband . . . So thinking, she was beginning to nod off when she came to a realization.

She had thought of *Yuko* as a dissociated and

unrealistic woman, but the real her was even more dissonant, so much wider, so much deeper.

But weren't all adults like that? Didn't they all observe their surroundings and act accordingly? Didn't they all take care not to make those around them feel uncomfortable? There was nothing strange about that.

Are you kidding me?

A child's voice resounded in her ears, as vivid and annoying as acrylic paint smeared on her fingertips. A young girl had said that to her while pushing her away in disgust. Who? A girl with dirty hands, a girl who had always glared at her. Right.

Tomoko.

She was standing alongside Tomoko on a narrow mountain path.

They were on their way to find the source of the river.

THE YOUNG OWNER of the soba noodle restaurant, being familiar with the mountain, led at the head of the group, while another adult watched over the children from the tail of the procession. Just in case, the children themselves had been assigned partners and had been instructed to take care so as not to get separated.

Her younger brother, a first grader, had been paired with a middle school student accustomed to mountain climbing, while Kinari, in third grade, had been partnered with her cousin Tomoko. Tomoko was three or four years her senior, with a large build and a spirited disposition, and had been instructed by both families to take care of her younger cousin, who had recently transferred to the same school.

"Everyone's making a huge deal over it, but it's actually really lame."

Yes, it was Tomoko who had said that to her. She had lived in this mountainous area ever since she was born, and it sounded like she had visited the headwaters of the river countless times before. She looked bored, dragging her feet as she walked. Every now and then, she would pick a small fruit from a nearby bush or branch and stuff it into her mouth with a familiar hand. Her fingers were always brown and dirty, stained with grime and plant sap.

"Here," she said, holding out three black grapelike berries.

Kinari was at a loss, uncertain how to respond, when Tomoko narrowed her eyes in annoyance.

She was never one to hide her displeasure. No sooner would she open her mouth than she would start cursing her hometown, calling it a cramped, lame, worthless country backwater, and then she would stare Kinari's way, trying to gauge the reaction of her newly arrived cousin whose father had just been transferred by his company from the big city.

"We'll be going back in two years, so don't pick up any strange habits, okay? And don't eat anything you find growing in the wild. The local kids might be used to that sort of thing, but it will give you a bellyache."

Her fashion-obsessed mother, having grown up in the city, hated the countryside with its mountains and rice fields. By *strange habits*, she probably meant the kinds of cruel games that were popular among the local children at the time, like breaking the wings of dragonflies or butterflies and throwing them into the cage of a friend's pet praying mantis, or using the hem of one's shirt as a grip to pull a grasshopper in half, leaving its severed head attached to the fabric, and competing over who could collect the most.

"No. No!"

She had to stop her brother from trying to tear off the heads of grasshoppers. It was her job to protect him from these *strange habits*, to make sure that he maintained a proper distance from the local children. She simply did what was expected of her as his older sister.

That was why the berries had caught her so off guard, leaving her racking her brain for an appropriate response.

Three seconds after she let her eyes wander—

"Are you kidding me?" Tomoko, still grasping the black berries, shoved her with all her strength.

Ah, Kinari thought, as she began to roll down the brush-covered slope.

"Yuko!" came her brother's muffled scream, sounding as though from underwater.

Her memory of what happened next was vague and patchy. The line of the other children spun farther and farther away. Her hands and face were coated in mud, and she was covered in cuts and bruises from some sharp bamboo grass–like plant. Her brother was crying. The young owner of the soba noodle restaurant came to help her back up.

In the end, they had still gone on to the headwaters of the river, so she mustn't have been too badly hurt.

When Tomoko started middle school, the town was rife with rumors about her dating a stranger—an adult at that—whom she had met on an online dating site. It sounded like she had even aborted a child from an unknown father.

At first, Kinari failed to understand which part of the rumor was so bad. Was it that Tomoko was dating someone without her parents' knowledge? That she was dating an adult while still a child herself? That she had aborted a baby? Kinari didn't know which part was worst, but the man was supposed to be older and more mature than Tomoko, so wasn't he the one at fault?

But as she watched the adults around her discussing her cousin, their lips curling slightly in barely contained grins, she began to think. Tomoko might have been a child, but she had a precocious and lascivious mind, even going so far as to lie to her parents to meet with a stranger. She was bad, she was soiled, and she wouldn't be able to marry anymore. Shortly thereafter, her family moved away.

Whenever Kinari thought back to Tomoko, a bitterness filled her heart. She was a typical country bully, violent, mean, and unrefined. It served her right that she had met with her terrible fate.

But why, Kinari wondered, had Tomoko had to hate *her* so much?

"SO DID YOU want to eat the berries? Or were you really put off by the idea?" Nowatari's voice was always gentle when he asked about her memories. No matter how unseemly her mistakes, he accepted them all with a gentle nod.

"I don't know."

"I think that's why Tomoko got so angry."

Less than two months had passed since they had moved to the countryside when her mother, finding several grasshopper heads crushed into the hem of her brother's shirt as she did the laundry, let out a shrill scream.

Though their mother scolded him like a raging tempest, her brother didn't stop playing with bugs.

He later collected a handful of swallowtail larvae and let them loose inside the house, hatched a praying mantis in his desk drawer, and caused various other incidents and quarrels with his parents, until finally he was permitted to keep as many insects as he wanted in an old fish tank in his room.

Her brother was uninhibited. He wasn't afraid to clash with others when there was something that he wanted to do. When it was time for his university entrance exams, he completely ignored his father's wishes and accepted an offer from a university in Okinawa. He stayed there after graduating and started working for a research institute dealing with environmental issues. He and their parents feuded for a long time, but once he got married and had a child of his own, their relationship returned to relative normality.

"My parents always like to complain that they can't get anywhere with him, but they both love him more than they do me. Tomoko didn't bully him either. I'm the only one she hated."

She had done her best to live up to everyone's expectations. She had worked hard. She had tried to be considerate of others. The more that she took care of their needs, the kinder that her parents, her parents-in-law, and her husband were to her.

So why did it feel like no one else in the whole wide world truly saw her for who she was?

A rippling laughter erupted from her side, filling the air of the hotel.

"People look down on things that don't threaten them. But you know what? *I* love you, your emptiness and purity. There's no one to claim you, no self to claim."

To Kinari, Nowatari was the only person who truly forgave her for being herself. She wanted to cry. Emptiness. Yes, her essence was that of a hollow cavity filled with water. Only the man lying beside her could love such a warped nature. Only he treated her with affection.

It was no longer rain that soaked her heart but an abundant river that took hold of her body, shaking her back and forth.

Nowatari flashed her a faint smile as he watched her linger in those waters.

She should have noticed. That his body, so close that she could touch it to her heart's content, wasn't wet with so much as a single drop.

The story of *Yuko* was featured in a special New Year edition of a literary magazine, then released in a short story collection three months later. It was a beautifully bound book, elegantly arranged with understated illustrations of flowers. It sounded like it had been favorably received, and it was apparently going to be reprinted.

Immediately after the work was first published,

Nowatari's invitations became increasingly infrequent, until by the time of the release of the short story collection, they had ended entirely.

That was when she first heard the rumor—that his wife had fallen ill, and he was busy taking care of her.

SHE DIDN'T EVEN need to use her prepared excuse, that she had forgotten to submit an assignment, to convince Yatabe to give her Nowatari's address.

With a newly released paperback and a box of sweets in hand, she made her way through town, the autumn breeze blowing around her. The sky had once been so blue that it had stung her retinas on those painful midsummer afternoons awaiting an invitation from her lover, but now it had become much lighter in color. A pale blue. A soft turquoise. The color of the rompers in which she used to dress her sons when they were babies.

She stepped onto the train, making her way to a station that she had only ever before passed through.

The rumor was that Nowatari's wife had left her husband, but what would she do if she bumped into her? She could say that she was a student from Nowatari's creative writing course and that she had come to turn in an assignment. She had heard that his wife was in bad shape, and so had brought the sweets as a get-well present. Leaning her head against the hand-rail on the train, she repeated the same ridiculous simulation over and over.

She might have seen Nowatari in class, but she hadn't met him privately for more than six months now. Even when she called him, he would turn her down softly, telling her that his wife was unwell and that he had a tight deadline approaching. Still, she couldn't give up hope. When his wife's condition improved and his difficult work was out of the way, there was a chance that they could once again let their *inner natures* intersect. All the more if his wife had left him. She couldn't quell this meager, twisted hope.

Just as she finished reading the new work, the train arrived at her destination. She closed the book, passed through the ticket gate, and made her way through the unfamiliar town.

Nowatari's home was a run-of-the-mill two-story house blending so easily into the residential landscape that she almost missed it. Was it newly built? The walls were still clean. She traced her finger across the name *Nowatari* engraved into the granite nameplate, her heart filling with joy.

When she looked up at the second floor, however, that sweet mood was scattered to the wind.

Green leaves were crammed up against the windows. What was going on?

That wasn't all that was creepy about the house. Even though it was located in the middle of a residential area, the empty plot next door to the Nowatari residence was overgrown with a dense thicket, the trees so tightly packed that it was impossible to see all the way into the mass of branches.

Kinari felt a shiver course down her spine. Something was happening to the Nowatari family—most likely something much stranger than the malformation that she harbored within herself.

Even after running through the situation so many times in her head, she couldn't bring herself to press the doorbell. Why not? Was this the guilt of a woman involved in an extramarital affair? But no, it wasn't that simple. Fear, yes, something close to raw horror, but which, for some reason, also made her heart race.

She tried again for a second, a third time, clutching her trembling fingers as she leaned against the guardrail opposite the house. She stared up at the quiet Nowatari residence. She couldn't know what was going on inside, but she had a clear presentiment. Nowatari's wife had rebelled against the love of her husband, who had besotted himself in the deformity of another woman with an affection that someone might have for a cherished butterfly collection.

And so, what was she to do? So long as this bizarre situation continued, Nowatari would remain obsessed with his wife.

All of a sudden, she noticed a branch of bell-shaped black fruit sprouting from the thicket. She approached it, touching one of those berries with her fingertips. They were as black pearls, round and with a glossy luster. They almost resembled blueberries, but they were much deeper in color.

So did you want to eat the berries? Or were you really put off by the idea?

Nowatari's gentle voice resounded in her ears.

Faster than she could think, Kinari threw a handful of those berries into her mouth, chewing through their tough skin with her back teeth. Their crushing sweetness, tinged with a hint of acidity, filled her jaw, the coarseness of their fine seeds spreading to the base of her tongue.

She held her breath and gulped them all down.

Together with the small birds that she sometimes saw in copses of wild trees but whose names she didn't know, Kinari continued to eat the fruit until her mouth was numb and her fingertips stained black.

3

THE MOMENT THAT SHIRASAKI KANON ENTERED
the room, her heart started pounding.

Green—no matter where she looked, there was
nothing but green. The space was filled to bursting
with overgrown grasses and trees. Leaves of every
shape and shade imaginable, some round, others
long and slender, gathered in her vision like clouds,
with a deep darkness accumulating behind them. It
looked like an unmaintained thicket on the outskirts
of town.

Tall grasses brushed against her stocking-clad
kneecaps. She felt a faint breeze blowing through the
room. There was enough light for her to make out
her surroundings without difficulty.

Her heart was beating so fast that she couldn't
hear anything else. Her numb body begged her brain
to make a decision. What *was* this? What was she to
make of it? Was she supposed to brush it all off, to
simply accept it?

She blinked as her thoughts tried to find something to latch on to, until they landed on the name of

her predecessor, Sekiguchi. Right, what was it that Sekiguchi had said?

"Mr. Nowatari's wife isn't living with him at the moment. She's moved away for one reason or another. You'll be meeting him on the first floor, so you probably won't even notice them, but don't worry about the plants upstairs."

Don't worry about them.

Those were her predecessor's instructions when he had handed over his old duties on the occasion of his transfer to the nonfiction department.

Right. *Don't worry about them.* That was what Sekiguchi, with his long career in general literature, had said to her. Her predecessor had been the power in the shadows when Nowatari Tetsuya won a local literary prize on the theme of love for his latest novel, *Garden*, released a half year ago. This was a considerable feat for Nowatari, who had been nominated for various awards in the past but hadn't actually been able to secure any of them. Unfortunately, it hadn't won the prestigious Akutagawa Prize after its magazine publication, but at the very least, its success proved that Sekiguchi Masashi's approach to managing the author was the right one.

That being the case, she shouldn't ignore his advice. Taking a deep breath, Shirasaki set foot in the dim forest. She followed the wall for three meters from the entrance, ruminating over his instructions as she pushed her way past the unkempt branches and waded through the tall grasses on her slippered feet.

Yes, when she stopped to think about it, writers certainly were an odd bunch. In the office, she had heard of one who showed up to meetings clad in a black kimono all year round, another who kept a pet donkey in his house, and one in particular who would call his editors at two o'clock in the morning to hurl abuse at them. There were countless strange rumors circulating about various authors, and in some cases, that strangeness was seen as a testament to their talent. Looked at that way, wasn't the fact that Nowatari grew a forest in his upstairs room simply a sign of the typical eccentricities of a writer?

So she said to herself, when a large bookshelf covered in moss suddenly emerged from the shade of a tree.

She felt like she was caught in a dream—a dangerous dream, the kind that might quickly turn into a nightmare at the slightest provocation. She sat down and peered at the bottom row of the bookshelf. *The Paintings of J. M. W. Turner*, *Maps of Edo and Old Tokyo*, *One Hundred Views of Showa Tokyo* . . . Ah, this was it. She laid her fingers on the top of the spine and carefully retrieved the copy of *One Hundred Views of Showa Tokyo*, followed by *Three Hundred and Seven Letters That Changed History* beside it. They were both big volumes, each almost ten centimeters thick, and quite heavy. She took them under her arm and made her way back through the strange forest.

No sooner did she close the door behind her than she found herself back in what looked like a regular suburban house. She was struck by vertigo. At the bottom of the stairs, she found Nowatari sitting bent forward on the sofa just as she had left him, staring at the blank notebook open in his hand.

"I found them, Mr. Nowatari."

"Oh, thanks."

"I think focusing on the early Showa era is a good idea. There are a lot of authors in their sixties and over who have written about it, but not many of your generation, so you might be able to offer a new perspective on—"

"Sorry, can you hold on a minute? I need to concentrate." His voice was gentle, but he was essentially telling her to shut up.

Feeling a numbness in her temples as Nowatari thumbed through the photo book, Shirasaki's mouth shut as firm as a ceramic figurine's. She was a rookie editor and had overstepped her bounds. Sekiguchi had warned her that once this author sank into concentration, she shouldn't say anything until he himself broke the silence.

The sound of pages turning. Nowatari's weak groan.

He hadn't written a single word in his notebook.

Shirasaki stared at her knees, peeking out from the edge of her flared beige skirt.

IT WAS THE doting boss from her previous department who had advised her to dress in a simple and plain manner. Almost twenty years Shirasaki's senior, her former boss had experience working in a wide range of departments, from general literature to advertising to fashion magazines, achieving positive business results in each of them, until just the other day, she had been promoted to the role of publishing director. She was a rare example of a female executive at the company.

"Most men, especially older men, don't really have much of a clue when it comes to the young women they work with. If you dress up in a stylish pantsuit, going on and on about your own opinions, they freeze up. Just like that, their minds slam shut, and they don't hear a thing. You're better off wearing a skirt and sweater or something soft that old men might like, nodding along to whatever they feel like saying while gently guiding them toward what you think is best with a few quick and considered comments."

In other words, that was how her old boss had navigated the complex web of company politics. She wasn't particularly attractive, but she always acted soft-spoken and placid of expression. No matter how busy she might be, she was attentive to those around her, and she had been accepted by the men of Yamairi Press as an ever-dependable maternal figure.

"I was also in charge of Nowatari for about two years a little after his debut. I remember him saying he gets along better with female editors, so you shouldn't have too hard a time of it."

That certainly seemed like a valid assessment. When she first met Nowatari in a hotel lounge together with Sekiguchi and the chief editor, Tanahashi, shortly after the former announced that he was changing departments, the author's expression had been calm and forbearing.

"My name is Shirasaki. I've been a fan of your work since I was a student. I'm honored to have the opportunity to work with you, Mr. Nowatari."

"Ah, Shirasaki. Which department were in you in previously?"

"Fashion magazines. Before that, I was in advertising."

"Hmm. Maybe that's why you have such a sophisticated look about you."

He smiled back at her, so at least she didn't get the impression that he had rejected her.

Then why wouldn't he let her offer him an opinion? Their meeting had already been going on for almost two hours, after all.

Had she made a mistake when she said that she was a fan of his work? Had he perhaps considered her too overzealous and unprofessional?

"SHIRASAKI, I DON'T suppose I could ask you to make a coffee? Everything you need should be in the kitchen."

It took a few seconds for her brain to process those words.

She must have looked like an idiot. No doubt wondering why she hadn't responded, Nowatari, who had been engrossed in his documents, suddenly glanced up at her.

"Coffee . . . Ah, yes, right away! Excuse me!"

All but leaping up into the air, she hurried toward the kitchen. She soon found a round and stylish blue-gray kettle, filled it with water, and put it on the stove.

Then she switched on the gas and let out a tired sigh as she waited for the water to come to a boil. She still didn't know exactly what was expected of a literature editor. Was this kind of domestic, secretarial work really part of the job? She wished that Sekiguchi had told her what she was supposed to do.

Ah, but if they were meeting at a restaurant or the like, she would almost certainly have ordered coffee. She should have been more thoughtful. With that in mind, she prepared a mug of drip coffee and brought it to the author.

"Huh? You could have made yourself a cup too."

For a moment, she didn't understand why he was laughing. Her eyes wandered for a second, until she realized that he must have been pondering why she hadn't made herself a drink as well.

"There's some chocolate in the fridge, so feel free to help yourself."

Was he being kind to her?

How exactly *did* Nowatari see her?

In the end, she brewed another cup of coffee for herself, sipping at it as she waited for the author to come up with something. An hour later, he shook his head. "I don't think I can do it today." And so their third meeting came to an end.

AFTER RETURNING TO the office with a heavy feeling in her chest, Shirasaki decided that she needed a change of scenery, and so headed for the company cafeteria. She made her order at the ticket machine, picked up her coffee at the counter, and took a seat at one of the many empty tables at the back of the room, whereupon she pulled a thick stack of papers from her tote bag.

It was the latest full-length novel manuscript by the emperor of horror suspense, whose popular works had been dramatized countless times over since his debut more than thirty years ago. While the editor assigned to him before Sekiguchi had convinced him to set out on this particular work, given that he wasn't an exceptionally fast writer, everyone had assumed that it would be a while yet before the company received a completed manuscript. As such, when his unexpected email arrived three days ago, Shirasaki had felt as though she was no longer treading on solid ground. She returned home in a daze and ended up huddling in the entranceway to read the entire thing in one sitting. She didn't even realize until her husband told her later that he had been forced to step over her when he arrived back after her.

It was a work of technique and passion worthy of the emperor's esteemed reputation, a human horror story revolving around folly and danger, pulling in a variety of contemporary social issues such as poverty and discrimination.

Nonetheless, it wasn't particularly interesting.

The first half of the work was engrossing, her heart throbbing at each new tragic event, but she had a hard time making it through the second half. When she reached the end, she wasn't moved so much as relieved that it was all finally over.

After reading the final page, Shirasaki was left dumbfounded, holding her head in her hands. As

painful as they would no doubt be to hear, she had to
let the emperor know her thoughts as quickly, and as
delicately, as possible. If possible, she should provide
him with a concrete written proposal for revision.

She annotated the manuscript with her thoughts
and met with Tanahashi to ensure that she had his
support. He fell to thinking for a long moment before finally muttering: "It's the second half here . . ."
When she agreed with him, he simply handed back
the stack of papers and said: "Yeah, so long as you see
the problem. This is all good experience for you."

Feeling sick to her stomach from the pressure being thrown on her, she repeatedly flipped through
the manuscript, already crammed with notes.

She must have passed around two hours like that.
Feeling a heavy weight behind her eyes, she looked up
to find Nasuno Tae, a colleague who had joined the
company at the same time as her and who currently
belonged to the paperback editorial department, eating a plate of omu-rice in the seat next to her.

Nasuno, noticing her movements, glanced across
at her. "You look like you're going all out there."

"You too. It's a little early for dinner, isn't it?"

"I'm helping out with an event tonight."

Pale and thin, with her light brown hair tied up
in a loose bun, Nasuno left a vaguely dainty impression that called to mind an image of flowers
and small birds. Yet in spite of that delicate and cute

appearance, she could be quite bold and daring. At one time, she had taken a work of literary fiction that hadn't sold well in hardback form and replaced its simple and elegant cover art with a piece by an up-and-coming erotic-grotesque illustrator to attract more attention to the paperback edition. Sales improved because of that, but she also stirred up a fair amount of controversy, earning herself friends and enemies alike.

"Hey, so about the commentary for Nirayama's paperback coming out at the end of the year, right? He and Nowatari are around the same age, and they often allude to each other's works, so I was wondering whether Nowatari might be able to put something together. Do you know if he's busy? You've taken over responsibility for him, right?"

"Ah. Yes."

Right, she couldn't forget about Nowatari. He was still at a complete loss when it came to ideas for his next work, and there was no indication when he would be able to have another manuscript ready. Shirasaki's head stooped further from the added weight.

"Not busy, exactly . . . Unwell, maybe. He can't seem to come up with ideas for any new stories, and it sounds like he hasn't taken on any work for any other publishers either."

"Huh. Did he burn out after *Garden* or something?"

"Maybe. Well, apparently he wasn't a very fast writer to begin with . . ."

As she spoke, she felt a bead of sweat begin to trickle down her back. No, that wasn't the only source of her unease. She knew that. This feeling of having dodged the question only made it harder for her to breathe.

"I mean, maybe I did something wrong. When we first met, I was so excited that I told him I've been a big fan of his ever since my student days. But when I had my meeting with him, he wouldn't say anything at all. I just sat there waiting for him, while he brooded over his thoughts all by himself . . . No, he *did* tell me to help myself to coffee and snacks, so he mustn't completely hate me . . . Ah, my stomach hurts."

"Hmm. So things aren't going too well?"

"Well . . . I guess you could say that."

"That's fine then. I'll find someone else."

Nasuno looked ready to change the subject, but Shirasaki quickly added a few more words: "No, maybe he's just angry at me. If you ask him yourself, Natchan, he might be fine with it."

"Do you think so?"

"Hmm, maybe. Anyway . . . I'll do my best to come up with some good suggestions and try to earn his trust."

Oh? Nasuno mouthed faintly, sinking back into thought. "I didn't know you were such a fan of his."

"Ah. Yes."

"Because of *Tears*, right?"

"Yes, that one really touched me right when I was going through a bit of an impressionable phase."

She had been a third-year university student at the time of its publication and was left deeply shocked by the work.

It was the story of a first-person *I*, an unsuccessful novelist, and his budding relationship with a woman known as Rui—written with the character for *tears*—whom he meets at a local bar.

Shirasaki was struck by Rui's innocent and endearing depiction and had felt a profound thrill while reading, quite as though she herself had taken on the role of the protagonist in the unreserved and graphic sex scenes. It was exhilarating to see a woman taking the initiative and engaging in sex with such joy and vigor, a refreshing break from the traditional stereotype of women being reserved and unaware of their own bodies, with sex being something to be stolen away from them.

She let her impressions spill out one after the other.

Nasuno nodded, pursing her lips. "Yeah, a lot of people like that about it. But you know, when I read it, I got the impression that Nowatari was only pretending to be an ally of women. It gave me this really off-putting vibe, you know?"

"Huh? What do you mean?"

"Why does Rui, who has no problem sleeping with all these men as a matter of course, only have sex with the protagonist once she's fallen in love with him?"

"That's . . . because she manages to satisfy the hunger for affection that she's lived with ever since her unhappy childhood, right?"

"Then why is it that he has so many male characters who are allowed to have relationships with all these women, but he has to go to the trouble of setting up a miserable childhood if a female character has similar urges, and then have his male protagonist ride in to save her?"

Flustered at hearing her favorite novel be disparaged in this way, she responded with a question of her own: "But if you put it that way, wouldn't the plot be all over the place? It would ruin the story."

After all, if Rui was to continue having her affairs after marrying the protagonist, the reader wouldn't have any sense of closure at the end of the novel.

"Ruin? I don't know if I would go that far . . . But isn't the point of the story to reach beyond that?"

"Sorry, I don't really see what you're getting at."

"It's the kind of story that everyone wants to believe. In that sense, Nowatari is an excellent writer."

"That doesn't really sound like a compliment though."

"It is. I mean it will sell. But I think you have to consider who the story is for."

Having finished her meal, Nasuno began to collect her belongings, picking up her cafeteria tray as she rose to her feet.

"Shirasaki, Nasuno! Sorry, can I borrow you for a moment?"

Glancing around at the cheerful voice, Shirasaki spotted Hataoka, a colleague of theirs in the sales department who had joined the company at the same time as she and Nasuno, running toward them with one hand raised. It seemed that a large-scale event was being planned for a new edition of a recently dramatized mystery novel, and the author and various individuals related to the television production had been invited to attend. The editorial department had been asked to assist. With no particular reason to turn him down, she took on the extra duties without objection, and so listened to a quick rundown of what was required of her.

"Are you in charge of it over at the sales department?" Shirasaki asked.

"No, that's Mr. Sasagi. I'm his sub."

"Alright. Email me the details when you get a chance."

Hataoka hurried off. It sounded like he would be busy for a while.

Nasuno, who had simply nodded along without saying much, suddenly grumbled: "Have you ever wondered why it's so natural for a man to drop the titles and call a woman just by her name, but we can't do the same to them?"

What a pain, Shirasaki thought. She stared down at her neat pale-lavender top and flared beige skirt. Her outfit was merely the result of careful consideration and planning. No matter how ridiculous it might have felt, if this was what reality demanded of her, she had no choice but to go along with it.

"I suppose dropping honorifics when addressing people *is* a stereotype of men's language. But I don't think he means anything bad by it, you know?"

"Of course not. If he did, that would be harassment. No, the problem here is that he *doesn't* mean anything by it." Frowning, Nasuno left the cafeteria.

RECENTLY, IT HAD become a habit of Shirasaki's to sit for a while in the doorway at the entrance to her apartment whenever she arrived home. In addition to the enormous and unfamiliar work that she had taken over from Sekiguchi, who had been managing nearly thirty separate authors, she still had a number of uncompleted projects from her previous position in the fashion magazine department. Not a day went past when she didn't feel overwhelmed by work.

But at last, another day was over. She slurped on the coconut-flavored bubble tea that she had bought from the convenience store in front of the station on the way home. This was the moment when she could most relax.

She was casting her gaze around the uneven wallpaper as she reflected on the events of the day when she heard the sound of the front door being unlocked. Her husband, Takao, entered, along with the smell of outside. He must have been tired, as his face was grim.

"Welcome home."

"Don't just lie there in the entrance. It's too narrow in here."

"Sorry. I was exhausted."

"So am I."

With a sigh, he strode over her in his wrinkled suit, disappearing inside.

She first met Takao, three years her senior, at a university seminar. The two of them had been together for close to a decade now. Two years after she graduated, with them both having gotten used to life in the working world, they decided that it was about time that they tied the knot, and so they just naturally ended up that way without either of them having properly proposed to the other.

"Have you eaten?"

"Not yet. I was thinking of doing something with the leftovers."

"I'll make udon. Do you want any?"

"Ah, that would be great."

Shirasaki sat down in front of the TV as she sipped at the bowl of udon noodles mixed with egg and spinach that her husband had made for her. There was a documentary playing, an inspection of the facilities at a British Antarctic research station. When she was working on a book, information that might seem at first to be of no relevance whatsoever could become suddenly useful, so she focused intently on the screen. Then, Takao, bringing his own bowl to the table, picked up the remote, and without so much as a second thought, switched stations to a variety show.

A torrent of sound came rushing into her ears.

"I was watching that."

"I don't want to watch something so boring and depressing after work."

As the show about a celebrity couple making fun of each other's lives played in the background, Takao popped open a can of beer and began to let loose with a litany of grievances about work: "That annoying bastard never asks anyone for help. He just puts everything off until the complaints start rolling in and the shit hits the fan. But because he's one year older than me, he gets a higher salary. So that's how my day ended, as the fall guy for that asshole. Seriously, I want to strangle him."

"Ah, I know someone just like that. They're such a pain." Shirasaki, staring at the edge of the TV, nodded along to her incendiary husband as delicately as she could. They used to get excited about all sorts of topics back when they had been students. They probably would have even enjoyed watching the documentary about the Antarctic research station together, exchanging opinions on one thing or another.

Takao's situation at work had deteriorated three years ago when he had been transferred to a new position. Until that time, he had led a fulfilling life in an advertising role for a major industry player— but when his boss, with whom he had maintained a strong working relationship, lost a factional battle within the company and was dispatched to a regional branch office, Takao too, widely regarded as his natural successor, was transferred to an administrative department in which he had absolutely no interest. It seemed that the department had become a dumping ground for useless employees, and so Takao, the newest member of the team, was left doing most of the work. The more that Shirasaki heard about it all, the sorrier that she felt for him.

That said, there was never any end in sight to his constant complaints. *Why don't you look for another job in the same industry?* But whenever she suggested that, he would always demur, saying that the people at the top thought highly of him and would eventually transfer him back to a more productive role. *When, exactly? What kind of position do you want? Since when did they have the right to transfer you in the first place?* Yet the more questions that she asked, the more that he glowered back at her with indignation. But he would offer no constructive opinions of his own to overcome his situation, merely spewing out his hatred for those around him. This had been going on for three whole years now.

At one point, he had all but rounded on her: "Why should I have to move to a lesser company? No matter where you go, they're all structured the same way. In that case, I'm better off staying where I am. The pay is a hell of a lot better than anywhere else, that's for sure."

Shirasaki rolled her eyes at the term *lesser company.* That concept didn't mean anything to her. Was his pride at working for an instantly recognizable industry force more important than alleviating the constant dissatisfaction and frustration of a job in which he could well end up trapped for the rest of his life?

She couldn't say that there wasn't a hint of disgusted astonishment to her gaze. Even if she did feel a sense of attachment to her work at Yamairi Press, at the very least, she wasn't blinded by pride. When she had set out job hunting in her final year of university, she had placed more emphasis on finding a company that produced the kinds of books that she liked rather than worrying about how big or prestigious they were.

What emotions did Takao read in her face? In any event, he gave her a dirty look and stood up without saying anything.

Since then, Shirasaki became hesitant to talk to him about the things that happened at her own job, good or bad. There was around a million-yen difference between their respective annual incomes. After subtracting what they both needed for their various living expenses, they transferred the rest into a shared family account, saving it for their future. Neither of them had any fancy hobbies or made any flashy purchases, nor did they have any reason to worry about money. For that reason, she had never been particularly conscious of the discrepancy between their salaries, and she had gone about her life as though the two of them were contributing equally.

But Takao might not have seen it that way. He might have been looking down on her for earning a lesser income at a lesser company. Such suspicions, once sprouted, were all but impossible to weed out, and so when the two of them sat down at the dining table, they only ever made idle conversation about whatever was showing on television, or else she would act as a captive audience for her husband's workplace complaints. Their relationship grew increasingly awkward.

Today, however, tired of simply nodding inanely along, Shirasaki changed the subject: "Oh, by the way, I went to Nowatari Tetsuya's house today. It was our first one-on-one meeting together."

Back during his university days, Takao had worked part-time at a bookstore. He had been such a voracious booklover that he would read the newest authors even before they had a chance to become breakthrough successes, and he would write the recommendation displays introducing new works as guaranteed future bestsellers. Nowatari was one of many such authors whose works he had introduced, and so she thought that he would no doubt find today's incident amusing.

Takao must have still remembered that time, as his eyes widened at the mention of Nowatari Tetsuya's name. "Oh? What was he like? A guy like that, I'll bet he's a total crackpot."

"A hundred percent. I mean, one of the upstairs rooms in his house is completely overgrown with plants. It's practically a forest. It was amazing."

A crackpot?

Did she really think that? What she had felt in that room was more akin to fear and loathing—but no, that was certainly proof of his genius. So her feelings must have been closer to dread and awe.

But for now, if it would help soothe Takao's pent-up anger, she would agree to call the author a crackpot.

Sure enough, her husband broke out into laughter. "Seriously? I knew he must have had a screw or two loose. I mean, what with all the attention that book *Tears* or whatever it was called brought to his wife? He even wrote about their sex life out in the open. But I guess it must have been all well and good if she doesn't mind that kind of exposure every now and then."

"Isn't that a sign of the respect that she has for her husband and his work? She knew that his job is to write about people, so she let him write about her own most personal experiences too. Don't you think?"

It was love, she thought with a sting. The Nowatari couple had devoted their lives to the art of the novel, peeling back their hearts and bodies, their flesh and bones, and exposing the dignity and shame that lay hidden behind everything else. Like so many other readers, she was struck by the authenticity of that unselfish professional ideal, by the depths of their unique and inimitable love for each other. A shiver of elation ran down her spine.

"I need to do my best too," she murmured to herself.

Takao shrugged his shoulders and said, his tone somewhat dismissive: "It must be pretty cozy, huh? I mean, getting paid to think about all that fluffy nonsense that people regard so highly all day? And here I am spending my days counting money and cleaning up after other people's messes." His voice was simultaneously both sulky and indulgent, a little light and a little dark, making it difficult for her to tell whether or not he was joking.

"It isn't all beautiful things though."

There were countless dirty, painful, unreasonable aspects to the publishing industry. The kind of trouble that arose when a certain number of people came together was probably the same no matter where you worked. But she felt that there wasn't much point explaining that to her husband right now.

Takao had changed. With each step—graduating from university, starting at his company, developing his career—he had transformed, little by little. The topics in which he was interested, the breadth of ideas that he was willing to accept, had become narrower and narrower, and everything else had become a target for his disdain. The fun-loving man with whom she had fallen in love as a university student, with whom she could freely share anything and everything, was no longer there.

But why, exactly, had he disappeared?

Unable to find an answer, Shirasaki waited for Takao to retreat to the bedroom, before downing a bottle of wine all by herself. Every time that she emptied her glass, her head felt somehow lighter, as though all the painful things that were too difficult to comprehend had faded off into the distance. She didn't know when to stop. Before she knew it, she was so drunk that she could no longer even find her feet.

THE SECOND TIME that Shirasaki visited the forest on the top floor of the Nowatari residence, she was met with a feeling not of awe or disgust but rather a strange sense of security. Her breathing deepened as she took in the scent of the trees, while her eyes and ears found the quiet, dimly lit space somehow soothing.

Holding her left hand to the wall, she waded through the undergrowth toward the bookshelf on the far side of the room. Today, she was looking for *Postwar Widows* and *Dancehall and Jazz Culture*.

She had prepared several potential themes in advance of their meeting, but Nowatari rejected them all. "I'm not in the mood for that kind of thing," he said. And so once more, she continued to wait on him until he struck on an epiphany. She gauged the best moment to brew a pot of coffee, unwrapped a box of sweets that she had brought with her, placed

it within arm's reach, and held her breath so as not
to disturb his thoughts. If Takao could see her, he
would probably fume that she was getting paid to do
little more than sit around and do nothing.

The only topic of Shirasaki's that Nowatari found
interesting was a family matter that she mentioned in
passing during their break. At the time, he was holding the book that she had retrieved for him the other
day, *Three Hundred and Seven Letters That Changed
History.*

"Oh, so your grandfather died in an accident
at sea?"

"Yes. My grandmother was in her fifties when
she lost him, but she kept writing love letters to him
for the next twenty years of her life, keeping them
all in an empty Morozoff cookie can. She lived with
my uncle and aunt, and when she passed away, they
found them with her belongings. There were close to
three hundred of them."

"That's a tasteful, touching story. Hmm. An accident at sea. That *would* make you want to write letters."

From there, Nowatari sank into thought.
"Showa . . . A Showa woman, maybe?" For the next
hour, he continued to mumble under his breath, until finally he landed on an idea: "A Showa-era ghost
story might work. I could go back to basics, maybe
base something around a woman's resentful spirit."
He had written several works set in the Showa era

and apparently had a good amount of reference material on it. And so, while he fleshed out this germ of a jumping-off point, he asked her to locate a couple of the books upstairs for him.

Why, she wondered, had he chosen to keep his reference materials in the forest room? It made them all but impossible to locate. She was forced to straddle the endless low-hanging branches and circle around bushes too thick to climb over. Given the layout of the building, the room should have been no larger than ten tatami mats in size, but no matter how far she walked, she could never reach the far wall.

Her toes, wrapped in the soft fabric of her slippers, crashed into something hard. She glanced down before letting out a small shriek.

It was a stone. A large, square stone, wide enough that she could have wrapped her arms around it. It was obviously cut by human hands and had been left lying there haphazardly. Its surface was dark in color and covered in moss, with small saplings reaching out from the fine cracks that crisscrossed its length.

A stone inside a house? And the kind of old stone that might have seemed more in keeping with an ancient ruin at that? Why? She squinted, glancing around carefully, only to find similar stones scattered all throughout the forest. She could see them amid the bushes, lodged into crevices, at the bases of trees, increasing in number deeper into the room.

Her first thought was that she shouldn't lift her hand from the wall. This room wasn't normal. She felt like she was trapped in a bad dream, that no matter how far she walked, she wouldn't move forward.

Have you ever wondered? The face of her coworker Nasuno suddenly came to mind.

In a corner of her memory, the lid of a beautiful cookie can lifted up, and three hundred love letters came pouring out.

During her final years, her grandmother hadn't gotten along with her son's wife, a working woman employed by a cosmetics company, and would often run away from home to spew insults to Shirasaki's mother. "That woman won't bear children, she doesn't do any housework, and she's as slovenly as a child herself." Her relatives had laughed it all off, claiming that she was becoming grouchy and taciturn with age, that she was old and stuck in her ways. But now that Shirasaki thought about it, her grandmother had been the youngest of five siblings and had grown old without ever having been given the chance to attend school or contribute to society.

Could she really interpret those letters as a beautiful symbol of love for one's lost husband?

The more that she pondered it, the stronger that the unpleasant feeling in her chest grew. Yes, she knew. She knew. Even outside this room, there were nightmares too elusive to grasp.

If it was no different in here than it was outside, what reason did she have to be afraid?

She took her hand off the wall and followed the stones.

As soon as there was nothing left to touch, her vision seemed to darken.

Relying on each new stone that rose out of the darkness to guide her path, she made her way into the heart of the forest. From time to time, she stole a look over her shoulder, but the walls were quickly obscured behind branches and leaves. As she continued to walk, the density of the surrounding trees began to diminish, until all of a sudden, there was a break in the foliage. She emerged into an open space almost like a public square.

In the center of it was a half-finished building made out of stacked stones. There was no roof or supports yet, and she could only make out the vaguest outline of its foundations, but she was struck by a clear sense of an individual's will and determination.

Someone was trying to build something.

A short-haired woman garbed in a white dress was sitting atop one of the stones, reading a book. She looked to be around twenty years old. There was a hint of innocence in her profile.

Unable to bring herself to fully believe that she had actually found someone in a place like this, Shirasaki fumbled to gather her scattered thoughts and called out to the woman: "Excuse me. What are you . . . Er, um, who might you be?"

The moment that she was able to make out the woman's face as she turned around, she felt a sense of déjà vu welling up inside her.

She knew this person. She had met her somewhere once before.

But she couldn't recognize her.

For her part, the woman didn't seem at all surprised as she lethargically moved her lips: "Who are you?"

"My name is Shirasaki. I'm from Yamairi Press."

"I'm Rui. Nowatari Rui."

Rui.

Rui . . . Rui—from *Tears*!

The letters flowed through her vision, coalescing into an image. The verdure called to mind the fresh and uninhibited wife of the first-person *I*. The woman sitting before her, from her cool face, her lithe body, her boyish manner of speaking, was exactly like Shirasaki's mental image of Rui from *Tears*.

"Rui! This is incredible . . . I love the novel you're in. I've read it so many times. I'm so happy to meet you."

She had spoken from the heart, but the woman's face stiffened, and she ran off into the depths of the forest.

Shirasaki stood still, watching on as that white dress vanished into the distance.

Had she done something wrong?

She stared at the stacked-stone monument. Now that Rui had disappeared, the forest was silent again. The branches and leaves, submersed in a thin layer of darkness, shrouded her surroundings.

Without warning, she lost all sense of direction, along with any confidence that she could find her way back. She had no choice but to keep following in the direction in which Rui had fled. Again, she trod through the grasses, winding around the bushes and breaking the branches that blocked her way.

A pale, red light oozed out from the shadows of the leaves up ahead. Squinting against the glare, she kept pushing forward, step by step. A fresh breeze blew in, as though a thin membrane had been stripped away, and the scent of raw earth began to waft through the air.

Before she knew it, she found herself standing at the edge of a thicket at nightfall. In front of her was a nondescript suburban residential area.

She glanced around, catching her breath.

Immediately beside her was the Nowatari residence.

The forest on the second floor was connected to the thicket next door. That strange space wasn't confined to a single room but had overflowed outside. Her arms broke out into goosebumps.

She made her way through the unlocked front door back into the living room before telling Nowatari that she hadn't been able to find the books.

"Oh. I guess I'll just have to buy new copies then," he said without looking up from his notepad.

THE WHITEBOARD SHOWING Sekiguchi's schedule indicated that he was on a three-day business trip to the Kansai region. Shirasaki left a message on his phone and made her way to the house studio where the photo shoot was scheduled to take place that afternoon. Shortly after midday, she received a call back. Was he on the bullet train? She could hear a mechanical engine-like sound in the background.

"That forest really is unusual, isn't it?" she asked, cutting straight to the point. There was a hint of anger in her voice over the fact that he hadn't properly explained the situation at the Nowatari residence during the handover.

Sekiguchi, on the other end of the line, clammed up for a few seconds before letting out a weak sigh. "Did you go into the room upstairs?"

"He wanted me to fetch him some materials."

"Oh . . . I suppose Nowatari *is* the kind to do that . . ."

"What exactly *is* that forest? There was a person in there. A young woman, with short hair . . . She called herself Nowatari Rui. She's his wife, isn't she? I thought you told me she had moved away?"

"Well . . ." Sekiguchi lapsed into silence once more.

The empty and unreliable quietude only made her ire seethe fiercer still. She wasn't upset at Sekiguchi—she was angry at herself.

What had been going through her head the first time that she set eyes on the forest? She had convinced herself that if Sekiguchi, with his long and successful career, wasn't concerned about the situation, neither should she be. And so she hadn't allowed herself to reflect on it any more than that. But neither the length of his career nor his age would convince her now that his assessment of it was in any way superior to her own.

She couldn't help but feel a wave of nausea coming on as that chain of thought buried deep in her consciousness broke free.

After a full minute of silence, Sekiguchi began to speak: "That forest . . . it was born from Rui. One day, she swallowed all these plant seeds. They started sprouting from her body, growing thicker by the day, until the couple's bedroom had been consumed by the forest."

"Why are you bringing up *Garden* all of a sudden?"

"I'm not. It's the other way around. *Garden* was based on what happened between the two of them . . .

Anyway, it's a problem for them to sort out. Our job is just to get manuscripts from him, so don't dig too deep into it. Do you hear me? Don't get too involved."

Despite his warnings, her mind couldn't see the connection between something as tangible as a manuscript and the elusive nature of that forest.

"But the forest on the second floor is connected to the outside. When I went looking for those reference materials, I got lost in it and ended up in the wooded area next door . . . It isn't a problem just for them anymore. It's completely spilled over."

"You've got to be kidding me . . . But she *did* say she wanted to go outside. I felt so bad for her . . . It isn't my fault."

"Mr. Sekiguchi?"

"We'll talk about it when I get back. Bye." With that, her irresponsible predecessor hung up.

As soon as she turned her attention back to the rain-soaked studio courtyard, her feelings conflicted, there came a sudden commotion from the entrance.

The first volume of essays by Mishima Tsutomu, a young up-and-coming actor, was due to be published by Yamairi Press shortly. The book was essentially a collection of articles from a popular section of the fashion magazine that Shirasaki used to work on, and to which Mishima contributed an essay and accompanying photographs once every three months.

The office had decided to keep her in charge during the serialization so as not to overburden the young actor, and so she was still tied up with this project even after her transfer. Once they finished the photo shoot for the cover artwork, she would be able to hand it over to his next editor. This was the final hurdle, she thought, steeling herself as she went to greet him.

"Thank you so much for coming today."

"No, thank *you* for arranging everything. Huh? Have you lost a little weight, Shirasaki? You look good."

"Eh? Thank you."

"Is this the dressing room?"

"Yes, just in here. We'll be doing the photo shoot in that room over there, and in the hallway too . . . Ah, I should check to see whether the photographer is ready."

Since they had worked together on so many different photo shoots, the preparations proceeded smoothly with no more than a light exchange of greetings and a few words of discussion with the agency staff and photographer.

In recent years, Mishima was often being cast in the roles of sweet, handsome men, or of eccentrics with outlandish personalities, and so his manager had suggested this essay collection as a way of showcasing a fragile boyish side. In order to give an impression of his private life, the studio had been set up in a traditional Japanese-style house with a lived-in atmosphere.

By the time that he stepped out of the dressing room after finishing his makeup, Mishima's mood had changed. The friendly aura that had greeted her just a short time prior had vanished, replaced now by one of nervous tension as he approached the designated positions. By turns, he sat down on the veranda, climbed the stairs, stood in the kitchen, and lay down in the living room. He didn't smile too much. His shoulders were relaxed, his gaze firm, yet at the same time, he exuded a vaguely wounded, restless impression. This was undoubtedly the so-called fragile boyish side that he had been cultivating.

The photo shoot wrapped up after around thirty minutes, and the staff began to put the equipment away. All at once, the actor's tense ambiance crumbled, and he flashed them all a relaxed smile. "Thanks, everyone," he said with a laugh, lighting up a cigarette and flopping down on the veranda like a cat.

Shirasaki watched on, feeling somehow reinvigorated.

That moment when an actor drops character. It was an ordinary scene, one that she had witnessed many times before.

There were people whose job it was to create beautiful illusions. And when that work was over,

they returned to being regular individuals. The illusion and the individual weren't one and the same,
nor were they under any obligation to be. Neither
Shirasaki nor anyone else involved in the project was
foolish enough to blame the actor for not actually
being the fragile boyish type. It was the same with
his fans. They knew that this fragile boy and the radiant princes whom he played were illusions, and
they enjoyed them for what they were.

Yes, the illusion and the individual were completely separate. She should have known that. Why,
then, had she equated Rui from the novel *Tears* with
Nowatari's wife?

She might have called out to her joyfully, but
Rui's expression moments before fleeing into the
forest was that of someone who had been doused
with icy water.

She had never so much as doubted that the woman
had allowed her husband to write about her openly,
just as Rui in *Tears* had offered her body to the protagonist with a bright smile. She had regarded such a
thing as possible.

But why?

Because it felt feminine to put emotion before
rationality, to fall madly in love, to surrender one's
own existence to support a man.

As she reached this conclusion, she broke out into
an unpleasant sweat.

She felt sick to her stomach. She lifted a hand to cover her mouth as the bitterness spread to her tongue.

If, for example, Mr. and Mrs. Nowatari's positions had been reversed, and it had been Rui who had written a tale based on her husband, she would no doubt have considered whether he felt uneasy about her depiction of him and would have then taken a half step back. The reason Nowatari hadn't done so was because Rui was a woman, because—without the slightest shred of ill intent—he bore an implicit prejudice against her.

The car arrived to take Mishima and the photography crew to the next site. After seeing them off, Shirasaki crouched down alone in the open entranceway, clutching her knees.

The rain grew heavier.

SHE WAS EATING the frozen pilaf and instant miso soup that she had bought from the convenience store when Takao, holding a vinyl umbrella, the shoulders of his suit dripping wet, walked through the front door.

"Welcome home."

"Ah, that smells good. What are you eating?"

"Pilaf. I get this urge to eat it every now and then. Do you want some?"

"I've already eaten," he said with a wave of his hand as he and his scent of earthy rain disappeared into the bathroom.

She finished her meal and quietly sipped her glass of wine. The television program was about the battle for survival between various animals that inhabited the Galápagos Islands.

Her husband, having changed into his pajamas after taking a shower, clutching a can of beer, was about to change the channel to a variety program when Shirasaki switched off the TV.

"Let's talk."

If they kept on living in separate worlds like this, she felt, they would both be ruined. Staring at her husband's face for the first time in what felt like ages, she realized just how tired he looked. And the person reflected in his eyes was undoubtedly suffering from a similar kind of exhaustion.

She sat down on the sofa and told Takao about all the unbelievable things that had happened to her since her transfer. How she had found an eerie forest in the Nowatari residence, and inside it, a woman.

"If that novel was so cruel and selfish, written without his wife's consent, what was I doing being so moved by it?"

Why hadn't she been able to distinguish between cruelty and beauty? She reread *Tears* after her encounter with Nowatari's wife, but on this fresh perusal, the work seemed to turn Rui into an eccentric, forcing on her the role of a punching bag whose sole purpose was to endlessly endure the protagonist's indulgences. Now that she had read it that way, she could no longer see it as the pure love story that she had once enjoyed.

There must have been countless opportunities for her to realize this before now.

Takao made a face, letting out a snort. "Consent? There's no such thing."

"There isn't?"

"It's do-or-die, this kind of thing. If she hated it so much, she should have beaten him to a pulp before he could publish it. Even after it came out, she could have gone public protesting against it. She should have tried publishing her side of the story, or suing him for defamation."

"Only a very strong person could do that."

"If you can't, it's over. Weakness sucks."

"So do you think it's normal for someone you love to write about you that way? How can you say that? It's obviously Mr. Nowatari who's at fault here, isn't it?" Shirasaki couldn't hide her displeasure at her husband's blunt manner of speaking.

A deep wrinkle appeared between his eyebrows. "You see, men are competitive right from the moment they're old enough to understand what's going on around them. They're always thinking about how to beat everyone else, how to show off their abilities, how to rise to the top. If you lose, that's it, you're a failure. You'll have to learn to accept that's how everyone's going to see you for the rest of your life. You know what I mean, right? No one loves a comic book hero who's weak right up to the very end. Only women can get away with being weak, without being condemned for it, without having to feel even the slightest shred of guilt. I can't relate to it at all, to be honest."

She frowned as her husband's words ran through her mind. "It isn't about men and women, it's about rights and human dignity! To start with, what's the point of all that competition? *That's* male society? What good is supposed to come if you win?"

To Shirasaki, it seemed obvious that life wasn't about competing with others but rather enriching oneself as an individual. She felt like her husband was an idiot for taking all that stuff about winning and losing so seriously. Not everyone could find happiness just by getting ahead in life. How many decades stuck in the past was he?

"Nothing," Takao continued, his expression serious. "Nothing good comes from winning. It's just a curse. A stupid, pointless curse. In the end, there's nothing left."

His eyes were as sober as could be. They were the eyes of someone who had recognized the curse, the sterile, unfertile pattern of thinking that ran deep within himself.

Shirasaki stared at her husband in a fresh light, as though struck in the chest by a soft force. A faint, strange, joy-like feeling washed over her. Painful to recognize though *it* was, her husband had seen through it.

They could talk. They could find a way to live with each other, in the same space.

After a short pause, Takao creased his brow, continuing: "But I know how it feels to be swept away by it. Nowatari Tetsuya probably thought he could write something amazing if he modeled it on his wife. He wanted to be a great and respected novelist. And that's all there is to it. There was no malicious intent involved. He probably never even had the opportunity to realize just how awful what he was doing actually was."

Shirasaki raised an eyebrow.

She didn't understand. No matter what one's career, no matter how strong their ambition to leave their mark on the world, how could anyone, without even having so much as a shred of malicious intent, do something so horrible as to take an individual's unique situation in life and process it into a work of art without their consent?

No matter how she pondered it, she couldn't reach the core of the problem. Takao, however, could see it. She and her husband might have been sitting close enough to touch each other if they just reached out, but an invisible glass wall stood between them—a cursed wall that couldn't easily be shattered.

But they could see each other. They had placed their hands against that wall, the both of them falling deep into thought.

"I want to live with you in a world where that curse has been broken, Takao."

"What kind of place is that supposed to be? It almost sounds like a dystopia, don't you think?"

She didn't know. She closed her eyes for a moment. What was there to love about someone once you stripped away those ideas of masculinity and femininity? She felt capable of drawing only a shallow, unrealistic image of whatever it might be.

"But I really like those other parts of you, outside of your strength," she said with all her heart.

Takao shrugged with unease, as though something had caught against his memories.

WHEN SHE SAT down in front of Nowatari at their fifth meeting, Shirasaki knew exactly what she wanted to say: "Please write the story of you and your wife."

Nowatari seemed bewildered, his forehead crinkling as a look of obvious dismay fell upon his face.

"What? There aren't always loaches under the willow tree, you know? I understand what you're saying, seeing as how well *Tears* and *Garden* sold, but I can't just keep writing about the same thing all the time . . ."

"I know. Your previous two works focused on your wife, so this time, I would like you to focus on you. Your feelings, your likes, the things that you've kept in and haven't yet written about in your novels. I want you to take your wife's perspective and think about how she sees the real you. And when you do that, what kind of conclusion do the two of you reach? That's the sort of story we need from you now."

"I can see how passionate you are about this, but just so you know, my wife is out of town for a while."

"She was in the forest upstairs."

Nowatari's eyes widened.

Soothing the nervous flutter in her chest so as to steady her voice and gaze, Shirasaki continued: "She looked like she was making something. So I thought you should make something too, Mr. Nowatari."

The air seemed somehow fresh and clean today. They might have been sitting in the living room, but she could smell the scent of greenery wafting through the building.

"Why don't you ever go into the forest, Mr. Nowatari?"

But Nowatari simply stared unmoving at the corner of the table, his mind already elsewhere.

Garbed today in bright magenta wide-leg trousers, she let out a deep exhale and leaned back into the sofa, her gaze falling on her knees. She was determined not to let this go, to wait, no matter how long it took.

The phone in her bag began to ring.

Nowatari, holding his forehead with one hand, didn't even glance at her. The display on her phone showed an incoming call from the emperor of horror suspense, to whom she had returned his manuscript complete with all her suggestions for revision the other day. "Excuse me," she said, retreating to the corridor. Resisting the urge to escape, she brought her breathing under control and pressed the answer button.

"Yamairi Press, Shirasaki speaking."

On the other end of the line, she heard a long exhale, followed by the heavy ring of a man's voice, low and shrill: "Ah . . . Er . . . It's Hachisuka. Were you the one who made all those notes in my manuscript, Ms. Shirasaki?"

"Y-yes . . ."

"You sure didn't hold back, did you? You're basically telling me to change the entire second half!"

Hachisuka's every word coursed painfully through her body. After all, he had been doing this for more than twenty years longer than she had, and his previous works were still enjoying regular reprints. She was afraid of upsetting him, afraid to offer her own opinion.

She and Hachisuka belonged to different generations, different genders, different environments, different everything. In the end, he would tell her to shut up, just like Nowatari. But this was her job. She had to say her piece.

"Um . . . I do apologize if I came across as rude. But since this is such an exciting manuscript, filled with all those excellent qualities that characterize your works, I feel as if the second half is a little overcrowded, and that you need to give each episode more space to breathe. I wouldn't want to see all that potential go to waste, so I hope you'll consider—"

"Why are you so jittery? My other editors haven't bothered to point out hardly any flaws recently, so I've practically had to edit everything myself. I like you. You're young, but you've got grit. Anyway . . . how does the end of the month sound? I'll try to get it back to you by then." Hachisuka ended the call with a joyful laugh.

Shirasaki let the hand holding her phone droop.

4

NOWATARI TETSUYA WAS STANDING IN LINE
at ten o'clock on a Wednesday morning waiting for
his local supermarket, Endo, to open.

The only other customers were elderly folk garbed
in dull-colored clothing and housewives clutching
reusable shopping bags in one hand. Nowatari was
the only man in his prime. When the automatic
doors finally slid open, he followed the flow of people to the deli corner.

The Endo supermarket had a thirty-percent-off
special on prepared food every Wednesday. The
kitchen was the centerpiece of the supermarket, and
popular items such as quiche and Nanban-style horse
mackerel tended to sell out within an hour of the
store opening.

Nowatari cast his eye over the mountain of indi-
vidually wrapped dishes and gathered those that he
had come to acquire with a practiced hand. Fried
shrimp and lotus-root fish cakes, braised eggplant,
ganmodoki tofu with spinach, seafood pad thai,
grilled shishamo, and assorted kimchi. After picking out close to fifteen packs in total, he deliberated

whether he should stock up on sake, beer, and whis-
key to pair with the food as he left the deli corner.
He also needed to buy milk, bread, and eggs. On top
of that, he was almost out of coffee, without which
he wouldn't be able to work at all.

He was peering down the aisle when a startled
voice sounded beside him: "Oh, Mr. Nowatari? Are
you shopping?"

It belonged to one of the students from his creative writing course. Her name was . . . Tanibe, if he
remembered correctly. Or was it Yatabe? She was a
housewife in her fifties. She loved to talk, had a bois-
terous laugh, and was always offering up a cheerful
smile. She had probably joined the creative writing
course simply to make friends rather than to hone
her storytelling skills. She always seemed most lively
when she got together with the other housewives after class over tea and coffee in the café on the top
floor of the cultural school building.

Come to think of it, she *had* said something
once about living in the same neighborhood as him.
Nowatari mechanically twisted the corners of his
mouth to return her smile. "Yes. I came to buy some
dishes."

"You've got a lot there, don't you?"

"I like to buy three days' stock at a time."

He had fallen into the habit of doing his shopping
twice a week—during the special on Wednesday and

the morning sale on Saturday. The Endo supermarket used seasonal vegetables in its prepared foods, and
the store frequently changed its lineup, so he never
grew tired of them.

It had been an everyday question, and he had
given it an everyday answer.

That was why, when Yatabe's face clouded over,
he felt like he had tripped over a pebble, his heart
skipping a beat.

"Oh? It must be hard all by yourself. If you need
anything, do let me know. I'm always happy to
talk."

What was so hard about being alone? Not knowing how to respond, he flashed her a vague smile. After all, the woman standing before him was a paying
student at his course, duly contributing five thousand
yen for each lesson.

"Thank you. I'll see you in class then."

After parting ways with Yatabe, he quickly put
the remaining items in the shopping cart and paid
the bill. Once outside, he stuffed his swollen shopping bag in the front basket of his bicycle and pedaled
home.

Back in his living room, he switched on the TV
and started a recording of a late-night travel show
that he had been meaning to get around to watching.
At the same time, he decided to have an early lunch,
preparing the fried shrimp and lotus-root fish cakes

with a pack of udon noodles that could be reconstituted simply by placing them under running water. The technology used to make chilled noodles had evidently become quite sophisticated in recent years. The package came not only with dipping sauce but also a serving of grated daikon radish, some chopped green onions, and a helping of wasabi paste in a small plastic package.

With a feeling of contentment, he slurped down the udon noodles and chewed on the crispy fried lotus-root fish cakes. The travel program starred two veteran male celebrities and a popular female announcer. The young announcer followed after the two veterans marching on ahead, paying the bill at the restaurants that they visited and providing information on the town. As he watched that buxom woman, endlessly smiling and taking care of the two men, he suddenly wondered why men who live alone were so pitied by those around them.

Ever since his wife Rui disappeared, the house had fallen into disorder. Sometimes, he would run out of toilet paper or laundry detergent right when they were needed most, and he would be left with no choice but to rush out and buy more. But that was just how it was. To be honest, he felt more comfortable living in a room that was perhaps a little messy, and he had no complaints about the store-bought food. He could always buy whatever daily necessities he needed at the large drugstore nearby. There was nothing wrong with living by himself.

But even so, if his parents or relatives could see him now, they would probably ridicule him for living like a sloppy teenager.

All of a sudden, his thoughts took him back to his parents' house, and he found himself blinking first once, then twice.

Did he still think of himself not as a writer but rather as the prodigal second son of the owners of a kimono store?

No, it was the way that Yatabe had looked at him, as though at something that didn't quite belong, that had aroused this nostalgic sense of irritation. Having reached this conclusion, he finished his lunch, scratched at his full stomach, and made himself a strong cup of coffee. He had to get around to starting on his next novel this afternoon.

His latest work, *Garden*, had won a local literary award and had been featured in the media several times. Thanks to that, he was receiving an increasing number of queries about his next one, but he had been unable to write anything at all.

He had a vague understanding of the reason why.

He was trying to move away from his stylistic tendency of using a female character as a medium for telling the story. Back when he first started out as an author, he had been an ardent fan of serious works revolving around male protagonists struggling in the face of various social and historical upheavals, and his early novels had reflected that sentiment.

They had not, however, sold well. At the time, he had lacked the technique and chivalrous spirit needed to strike success. No matter how badly he wanted to feature a protagonist endowed with a refined iron will, he couldn't work out how to incorporate one into a story in a compelling way.

It was at that time, while he was struggling to find his way, that he met Rui, got married, managed to loosen his shoulders a little, and wrote *Tears*, his first romance novel and an unexpected home run. Thanks to that work, he had managed to solidify his reputation as a writer, but now it had become difficult for him to break away from the style that it had established for him.

It wasn't that he disliked romance novels. It was simply that, having been born a man, he was driven by an unquenchable desire to write not only domestic tales about families and couples but also grand narratives revolving around tenacious individuals who could weather impossible storms entirely by themselves.

Nonetheless, he was finally on a roll. He couldn't afford to alienate his readers by putting out something half-baked. Even if he was to switch to a more hard-boiled style, he would need to inject just the right amount of those elements that had been so positively received in his romance novels. But that raised another problem. The sequence of romance novels that had started with *Tears* had reached a natural culmination with *Garden*, which focused on a woman reduced to despair over her relationship with a man. Was there anything left to write about after that? And if so, *how* was he to write it?

He cleared the dining table, lined up some reference materials that he hoped might prove to be of use, opened his notebook, and fell to pondering. He chased after the images that flashed through his mind, identifying the skeletons of various stories that had impressed him in the past, trying to reassemble them into a cohesive whole, but he couldn't quite grasp the tip of that radiant dragon's tail.

Why don't you ever go into the forest, Mr. Nowatari?

Perhaps because he was consciously trying to expand the range of his thoughts, a question that his young editor had asked him several days ago resounded in his ears.

There was no particular reason. On the contrary, why *would* he go in there?

Rui had allowed herself to become a forest. Probably out of suspicion that he was having an affair. Why should he have to chase after a woman who had so clearly rejected him? As he watched her undergo that transformation, he had written about the limits of love in *Garden*. And with that, it was over.

Or so he had thought—but then his editor claimed to have seen her in the forest.

He would have been able to accept it if Rui, despairing over their relationship and the endless differences in perception between men and women, had simply disappeared from the world. Since the dawn of history, there had been countless pitiful men left widowed by the deaths of their beloveds. He had even fantasized about how such individuals must have felt.

However, the possibility that she still existed, that she could be thinking something, that she could be doing something without his knowledge, stirred up complicated feelings of frustration inside him. He felt like he had been fooled into believing that the story was something that it wasn't.

He couldn't put the image together. Hearing about Rui just made him even more confused. He let out an exhale before glancing out through the window. It was growing dark. He had been deep in concentration for close to six hours.

He stretched his stiff back, picked up his wallet, changed into a fresh pair of clothes, grabbed a towel, and left the house. He hadn't been getting much exercise lately, so he decided to stop at the gym at the local health center to loosen up and then to go out for a drink.

As he started walking, he suddenly noticed the plot next to his house. He had secured the land with the intention of eventually building a separate work-space, but now that Rui was gone, that prospect was no longer in the cards. He had held off from letting go of it after the real estate agent informed him that, given the topography, it would be difficult to sell un-less it was combined into one unit with the house, but he would still have to think about how best to put it to use.

That aside, while he might indeed have neglected it, he couldn't help but wonder how a vacant lot could be so quickly overrun by such a dense thicket. As far as he could remember, it had seemed to be just a regular empty piece of land one moment and then covered by lush greenery the next. But it was also true that, at Rui's suggestion, he had at one point planned to build a garden there, a place where he could go to catch his thoughts, so perhaps it wasn't such a big problem after all.

On his way to the health center, he noticed a group of maintenance workers pruning the shrub-bery by the side of the road. Looking closely, he could see that plants and trees had sprung up all throughout town, their vigorous branches and leaves overflowing even from the frames of nearby buildings. In many places, the plants on the eaves of various structures had begun to overhang the road. They were clearly safety hazards.

He was struck by an indescribable feeling. It might have made sense if it was the height of summer, but it was already deep into autumn. Was this year's strange weather responsible for this explosive growth?

To top it all off, the maples lining the avenue adjacent to the health center were being cut down en masse. He was at first taken aback that those maples, which the townspeople so adored, were being removed, but when he looked carefully, he saw that the workers were carefully digging up the roots of countless other trees sprouted from the soil where the maples were planted. The sight of those trees all but suffocating the maples, of every color and thickness imaginable, was nothing short of bizarre.

Had it been like this the last time he went to the gym? Right, it must have been the week before last. He couldn't remember.

"What the heck is all this?" he called out to a member of the logging crew.

The worker, a middle-aged man with a sunken cast to his face and a white towel wrapped around his head, shrugged. "Beats me. The whole town is like this. Could be there's something wrong with the soil microbiology. Maybe it's an unusually fast-growing invasive species. Or maybe the rain changed this year . . . A bunch of scientists came to check it out the other day. Anyway, they keep growing back no matter how many times we cut them down," the man said tiredly as he resumed his work.

For a moment, Nowatari stood in awe at the sight of the ferocious growth in one of the plots that the workers had yet to reach, then entered the health center.

He took a shower after working out for an hour or so, then made his way outside. The sun had completely set. Now, where should he go to drink? He could try dumplings, or Italian, or grilled chicken skewers, or maybe Chinese. Pondering his options, he started walking in the direction of the station. The workers were calling it a day with half of the trees growing amid the maples yet to be removed. It was probably too dangerous for them to keep going at night, unable to see what they were doing.

With the sun having set, the overgrown trees resembled clumps of raw darkness. They were like fountains in slow motion, endless energy erupting up from the earth and pouring into the sky. Their leaves swayed in the gentle evening breeze.

As he stared at those masses, the darkness seemed to swell larger and larger. He hurried away.

He headed for the station. He finally caught his breath amid the miscellaneous streets lined with red lanterns and handwritten signs, and so hunted

around for today's haunt. Perhaps his eerie imagin-
ings were to blame for it, but he was in the mood for
greasy junk food.

After a short pause, his sense of reason dismissed
the idea of a restaurant that his tongue remembered
with a certain relish. It was a small izakaya bar run
by a middle-aged couple, with a pair of tables set up
on the terrace by the railroad tracks. The food was
good—baked potatoes with butter and salted fish,
fried chicken flavored with chili pepper, and a variety of other rough but tasteful dishes.

Nonetheless, it would be difficult for him now to
return to that restaurant.

None of the establishments appealed to him. Before he knew it, he had gone as far as the end of
the main street. Left with no other choice, he made
his way to a familiar Chinese restaurant and filled
his stomach with dumplings and green onion ramen
noodles.

A sigh escaped his lips as he stared at the old tables
and their peeling paint.

He knew that he had to get serious about starting on a new work. He was managing to keep rel-
atively busy thanks to all the promotional activities
for *Garden*, his column, miscellaneous book reviews,
and requests to write commentaries for other works,
but his sense of discomfort was beginning to come
to a head.

With Rui gone, his life had become much sim-
pler. His food and living expenses didn't add up to
much, and with no plans to have children or build
a separate workspace, he could afford to put the majority of his continued income from *Garden* into his
savings. He would still have to pay off the mortgage,
but so long as he was by himself, he wouldn't need to
put much effort into maintaining the house, and he
could always sell it if worse came to worst.

In Rui's absence, a burden had been lifted from
his shoulders. His spirit rejuvenated, new ideas
flowed through him without limit, and he began to
drift freely from one to the next. After all, women
were dead weight. Whenever they opened their
mouths, they would always insist that they were in
the right, and they would impose their own heavy
concepts of life, livelihood, love, duty, and whatnot
on everyone around them. They practically beat
a man to death with it all. They didn't provide a
space where you could easily belong, somewhere
like a Sunday park where you could transform into
a superhero by the mere act of jumping down from
some high place.

But that was probably fine. It was precisely because of the self-righteous oppressive weight that he
could measure whether he was good or bad, floating
or sinking. It might have been fun to keep playing
in the park forever, but it was scary when the sun

went down. No one would notice he had become as ephemeral as a ghost.

Now that he had lost the weight of a woman, if he didn't at least write a manuscript, he felt like the man whom he had worked so hard to create, Nowatari Tetsuya, would simply fade away. He wanted to write. He wanted to start writing *something* again so he could feel at ease.

But he couldn't find a way into a story. Even when he was walking down the street, training in the gym, or slurping a bowl of ramen noodles, his next novel was always in the back of his mind. But no matter how he struggled to start jotting down the opening to a grand epic, it would collapse into banal sterility after just the first few lines.

Instead, whenever he closed his eyes, what he saw was Rui, no longer human, rambling incoherently that she loved him—and that was precisely why she couldn't forgive him.

It was an intriguing sight. Unforgettable. He even felt his own chest tightening in affection.

Romance novels, in his mind, were the domain of women writers. It was one thing for a man to write one or two to showcase his ability, but it was essential for him to have a more concrete sensibility, a greater technical mastery or social outlook. Whenever he received praise for *Tears* or *Garden*, his chest choked simultaneously on both joy and bitterness.

No, he wanted to respond to such comments. Those works had simply been opportunities for him to catch his breath. His quintessential writing style was completely different.

But try as he might to resist, it seemed that he still couldn't escape from Rui's shadow. If she was preparing something deep in that forest, he had no other choice. For him to embark on another work, he would have to go in and retrieve her.

He washed the greasiness out of his mouth with a glass of lemon-infused ice water, and with a strained grimace, stood up from his table.

WHEN HE OPENED the door to the second-floor bedroom, the first sensation to wash over him was one of tedium.

Why did he have to go through all this trouble? Everything about it—from the dense trees blocking his view to the weeds tangling around his legs— reminded him of the night of his living room quarrel with Rui.

Why? Why do you need to do that? She had hurled those unanswerable questions his way like a hail of bullets, leaving him silently stricken with discomfiture and guilt. Forgetting the trivial promises of everyday life, going out for drinks with an acquaintance when she was ill, adapting the things that she did and said as material for his novels, letting himself get carried away every now and then and having a little extramarital affair—he certainly wasn't proud of those things, but when asked why they had happened, he could only respond that they simply had. *Why? Why? Why? Why? Why?*

There were times when all those *whys* that the woman hurled at him carried an almost barbaric ring about them. She was practically ordering him to dissect himself and remove those unsightly parts from his own flesh. They implied an unconscious arrogance, as though she believed that a human being could be composed of righteousness alone. In the end, dealing with her became so exhausting that he would shut himself away in his study and bury himself in work. The sound of her cries echoing down the corridor from the other room truly grated on his nerves.

The forest in front of him was filled with that same late-night gloom. It was a place that he didn't want to remember, a place that permitted neither sleep nor escape.

It was all too much.

He crouched down by the doorway leading into the bedroom and stared into the quiet forest. The scene in front of him might have been indoors, but it was strangely bright, enough for him to see several meters ahead, with a slight breeze wafting through.

The window at the back must have been open.

Right, he remembered seeing it from the outside what felt like so long ago, but the lush vines and leaves had soon spilled out from the frame, obscuring the window itself.

There were no insects in the forest, no animals— no signs of any life at all. And yet it was unmistakably breathing, trembling, expanding. What on earth was living in here?

The answer was obvious—Rui.

Walking into the forest meant entering her very interiority.

He didn't want to go. She would just hurl more well-deserved criticisms at him that he wouldn't be able to answer.

Ah, but he had to. Without her, he couldn't write his manuscript.

With his hands in his denim pockets, Nowatari arched his back and headed into the forest.

He regretted it almost immediately. How could a ten-mat room feel so ridiculously large?

Though it should have been no more than a few simple steps from the entrance, no matter how far he walked, straddling over bushes and ducking under branches, he couldn't reach the bed. All that he could hear was the sound of his own breathing and the rustling of leaves as he moved from place to place. It was enough to slowly paralyze his sense of the passage of time.

There soon came a break in the monotony of the forest. In the midst of that swarm of organic matter composed of soft and at times aggressive curves, a mass of straight lines cut into his vision with a clear sense of will as an easily recognizable man-made object appeared. It was a staircase, around two meters wide, built from old stones. And it went down.

There was a staircase in the forest?

No, the bedroom was on the second floor of the building, so it wasn't surprising that it would lead down, but it was hard to imagine where exactly it might go. Certainly not to the kitchen or living room.

Most of all, it was terribly confusing to suddenly find a stone staircase inside what he had recognized visually as no more than a mere forest. It suggested something underneath where he was standing, some form of structure.

He couldn't make out what lay at the end of the dark stairwell. But given what his editor had said, this staircase must have been what Rui was building. Frowning, he placed his hand against the wall and began to trudge downward. The pale light of the forest faded away as he sank into a darkness so deep that he couldn't even make out his own fingertips. He could discern a sound—the steady rhythm of a piece of heavy machinery moving into the distance.

He would normally be able to recognize such

sounds immediately, but for some reason, his mind was unusually sluggish. After taking a few more steps, he suddenly realized what it was—a train.

Yes, he remembered coming home by train one day after one of his meetings. Exhausted, he had debated with himself whether to stop somewhere for a drink.

He continued down the steps, one, two, three at a time, until he found himself in the stairwell leading to the ticket gates at the nearest subway station.

Under the magenta sunset, busy figures shrouded in faint shadow were coming and going in front of the station. Pulled along by an invisible thread, he made his way to a local izakaya bar by the railway tracks.

He slipped past the makeshift tables and the upside-down beer cases used for outside seating and entered the building. It might still have been early in the evening, but the establishment was crowded with customers. There was just enough space at the corner of the counter.

When he pulled out the stool and sat down, a plump, middle-aged woman wearing a black apron brought him a hand towel. Unable to make out her voice as she told him the names of today's recommended dishes, he waved the woman away, muttering that anything would be fine. On the other side of the counter, the reticent master of the house was deep-frying some food.

A young woman carrying a tray stacked with glasses of beer and sours appeared behind the older woman. She was wearing a white T-shirt and jeans along with the same style of black apron as the middle-aged woman. She had a slim build, but her toned body caught his attention, prompting him to imagine a pleasant sense of elasticity. She could have been a sportswoman, except he already knew that she wasn't. The kitchen in this cramped establishment was so small that she was forced to peel vegetables crouching down with a bowl on her lap. He remembered her laughing as she explained that working down on her knees and lifting and lowering all those ingredients made for a rigorous workout.

The woman was Rui—twenty years old, still with traces of a girlish innocence about her. He used to come to this izakaya bar every night to flirt with her. The middle-aged couple who ran the establishment couldn't resist the distinction of an intellectual cultural figure. He might have been considerably older than Rui, the daughter of a relative who had died of illness, but they were happy to approve of his relationship with her.

He couldn't recall what they had had to eat or drink. He had said that anything would be fine, so it must have been something appropriate. All that his body could remember was a vague sense of fatigue, a feeling of being fully satiated by the food and drink.

The customers in the bar gradually disappeared, until he realized that the owner and his wife were standing beside him with Rui, each of them watching him with equally inscrutable expressions.

It was the woman in the black apron who, with a shrug of her shoulders, spoke up first: "I don't know how to say this, Mr. Nowatari, but we're in a bit of a pickle here . . . We've had a lot of, well, I suppose you would call them stalkers, hanging around lately. Of course, everyone is always welcome here as a customer, you know? But we've had a lot of photographers come to take pictures in secret, asking all our female customers if they're Rui . . . Just today, one of our customers was in tears, saying she wouldn't be able to come here anymore. Besides . . ."

She was saying that she didn't want Rui to work there anymore. The older woman was dissembling, but he knew what she meant. She had already suggested as much several times before.

Hold on, he thought, stopping himself there. This exchange had taken place sometime after they had gotten married, after *Tears* had been released in paperback. Everything was connected, but it was all out of order.

When they started their new life together, Rui had moved into his small one-bedroom apartment. Their life was a portrait of poverty. To put it simply, their home was too small. He couldn't write at all while Rui was around, so he appreciated having her out of the house between noon and midnight. In that sense, it was extremely convenient to him for her to keep working at the family-owned bar.

"With all due respect, and as I've already explained, this is a matter of basic literacy. Even if my work isn't prefaced with a message pointing out that it's all fiction, it's obvious to the average reader. Otherwise, we would have mystery authors committing murder nonstop and romance novelists having affairs left, right, and center. But that doesn't happen. Still, the second you describe a town or a character's workplace, people start jumping up and down thinking that it's all based on your real life, and they even start poking their noses into your wife's business. It's crazy. Why should Rui or I have to change how we live just because of people like that? You should report them to the police. Besides, no book sells forever. It will all die down soon, and idiots like that will stop coming."

"B-but aren't they turning it into a TV miniseries? If we end up getting any more curious visitors . . ." The middle-aged woman turned to her husband, beseeching him for help.

Her behavior struck Nowatari as both borderline ridiculous and vaguely nostalgic. She was acting like a frightened raccoon dog.

When it came to couples of the older generation,

Nowatari was of a mind that most wives were merely ventriloquist dolls of their husbands. The only things that came out of their mouths were diluted versions of their husband's opinions and views with an added dose of public opinion—they didn't have any perspectives of their own. When an outsider brought those views into question and reality came crashing down on them, they reacted like helpless circus animals that had failed to perform. There were various kinds of reactions, ranging from anxious fumbling to a stubborn refusal to accept the blindingly obvious, but what they all had in common was that they were always looking out for the well-being of the hand that pulled the strings.

Unlike the middle-aged woman, who was visibly upset, Rui glanced from her foster parents to Nowatari as though she hadn't yet realized that they were talking about her. Nowatari appreciated her innocent nature. She was free-spirited and unbound by the trivial promises of the prior generation. She had a freshness that reminded him of a newly hatched cicada or butterfly.

Women were easy to deal with. They might complain every now and then, but they never thought to attack him head-on. Nonetheless, there was another troublesome existence before him.

"You're spouting some confusing malarkey there, but do you really need such a highfalutin excuse to take care of your wife? You've got money, don't you? Don't make her slave away in this cheap old dive. Take her home, put a baby in her, and let her raise it in peace, you hear me?"

If you don't do that, you're a coward, the man's rough, crushing tone of voice all but declared.

If Rui was going to stay at home, they would have to move, and if they were going to consider a place where they could raise a child, it would be better to buy instead of rent, but that would take a sizable bite out of his savings. He had been trapped in a long slump after his literary debut, and now that he had finally been blessed with a success, he had hoped that he might be able to have a little fun.

You've been using her as free labor all this time, but now that a few idiots are causing a nuisance of themselves, you're going to throw her out onto the street? Or so he wanted to say, but instead he fought to hold his tongue. These kinds of idealistic arguments mixed with a generous serving of contempt were difficult to rebuff through mere words. If he tried to use logic, he risked being laughed off. As he swallowed his voice, the middle-aged woman nodded in satisfaction, turning with a look of gratitude to her trusted companion. It made his stomach seethe with exasperation.

And so he had no choice but to ask how Rui might draw her time working for them to a close.

As they walked side by side on their way home from the establishment, Nowatari caught a peek of Rui's youthful profile. She had a refreshing, pale countenance, the kind that wouldn't let him read her emotions.

The fact that she was showing him this scene from the past must have meant that she hadn't wanted to quit her job. But if that was the case, why hadn't she said as much at the time? Nothing was going to come from her dredging it all back up at this late hour.

"Are you happy now?" His voice was tinged with weariness, all but chastising her for having forced him to relive these unpleasant memories.

Rui's eyes opened wide, and she took off at a run. She darted away without even the slightest hesitation, like a startled rabbit.

"Hey!"

The back of her white T-shirt disappeared down the stairs to the basement of the building that housed the restaurant. Biting back on his irritation, he chased after her.

The hard, dense concrete stairs beneath him faded into something else as he made his way down into the hollow cavern, the soles of his feet registering the feeling of soft wood.

The soles of his feet? He glanced down at his legs in consternation only to find that his shoes had disappeared, leaving just his white cotton socks. The narrow wooden staircase stretched into the distance, with only a faint light up ahead.

Nowatari continued downward.

HE FOUND HIMSELF on the first floor of his family's kimono store, Matoiya.

A schoolgirl in a sailor uniform and with a sharp but beautiful face stood at the entrance, shrugging her shoulders uncomfortably.

Ah, he couldn't even remember her name anymore.

Nowatari reflexively contorted his lips into a smile and pointed to the second floor.

"It's alright. Let's go."

"Maybe we shouldn't . . . What will your family think?"

"What's the matter? Come on. It'll be fun. Let's go."

He took the girl's hand. Right, he remembered, this was the first time that he had ever touched her. He had been so overjoyed. The girl had a reputation as the unruliest of her grade, yet her hand was silky like a brand-new bar of soap and easily fit into his own. He gave it a light squeeze and gently guided her upstairs. Only then did he realize that he was wearing the black stand-up collar of his old school uniform.

The Matoiya was a small three-story store on the edge of the wholesale district. The first floor was taken up by the cash register and accessories, the second was a fitting room for customers trying out kimonos and obi sashes, and the third served as the warehouse. The store was closed on the first and third Thursdays of each month, and Nowatari took advantage of those hours when his parents were out to meet customers or acquire new stock to invite girls from school to the fitting room on the second floor.

The walls of the spacious tatami-floored fitting room were lined with paulownia chests filled with clothes and equipment. The shelves were stacked with fabrics and accessories, and an ornate patterned kimono had been draped over a clothes rack, all probably in anticipation of the first customer tomorrow morning. On the other side of the room were dozens of rental kimonos hanging from a tension rod. The room was always filled with color, and the girls he brought here, overwhelmed by that elegant atmosphere, were usually rendered breathless as soon as they laid eyes on it.

"Come on in. Don't be nervous . . . That's it. Let's start with some light colors. Ah, but with your sharp and cool face, some deep, mature hues would look great on you too."

He pulled a couple of kimonos from one of the chests and draped them over the girl's shoulders in

turn. Ever since he was a child, Nowatari had pos-
sessed a rare ability to intuit what kind of clothes and
mannerisms would best help a woman to be seen at
her most attractive. Even before he was old enough
to go to kindergarten, he would scamper about his
mother as she fitted customers, suggesting this obi
sash or that one, this accessory or another, and his
mother would pat him on the head and commend
his sense of taste. On the other hand, his brother, six
years his elder, had an active personality that relished
the outdoors, and as a child, had been more interested
in robots and monsters than traditional kimonos.

After choosing a kimono and obi, he began to
remove the girl's school uniform, fitted her with a
loaner undershirt and hem coverings, and proceeded
to dress her quickly. All the while, this tough-acting
girl stood there as though in a waking dream. He
remembered fitting her with a refreshing white *Edo
komon* kimono that called to mind a clear autumn
sky, along with a mulberry-colored obi embroidered
with a silver-gray floral pattern.

"Isn't it a little odd, you fitting kimonos like this?
I mean, you're a man."

She probably felt embarrassed to have him touching her body, even if through clothes, but she nonetheless obediently raised her arms up into the air and
followed his every instruction.

"Don't be silly. There are a whole lot of male

kimono stylists involved in period dramas and ka-
buki theater and whatnot. My dad helps out at the
local theater sometimes too, you know? You need
a man's strength to tighten an obi so that it doesn't
come loose. Then again, I guess we'll be taking it off
pretty soon though."

Girls tended to react in one of two possible ways
whenever he said this. Some would be angered by his
suggestive tone of voice, while others would grow
only more bashful. The latter group might give him a
chance afterward, perhaps even allowing him to softly
touch their bodies once they had finished the fitting.

With her obi tied behind her, her hair done up,
and a light rouge on her lips, the girl was more attractive than he had ever seen her before. Her mod-
esty, stemming from her lack of familiarity with the
new attire, was the deciding factor. From Nowatari's
point of view, the behavior of a great many women
tended to start turning artificial and contrived once
they developed even a half-formed knowledge of kimonos. They would develop a certain coquetry, an
insufferable desire to be seen this way or that. What
he wanted was to bring out the natural beauty of
their bodies. Besides, there was something exciting
about rewriting the stories of girls his age, of transforming them into delicate flowers. It had a sensuality more corrupt and immoral than the physical act
of sex.

"You're beautiful, really."

Dressed as she was now in the kimono, those words that would have sounded hollow while she had been wearing her school uniform escaped from his lungs with heartfelt sincerity.

The girl's lips twitched in embarrassment.

He stood back for a moment, taking a photograph with the instant camera that he had asked her to bring, before, overcome with regret, he began to untie the obi.

"You know, Nowatari . . ."

"Hmm?"

She twisted her body as she turned around, pressing her lips up against his own. With a laugh, he warned her to be careful not to crease the fabric as he breathed in her vermilion scent and began to remove the kimono. She purred like a kitten as he squeezed her through the cloth and reached for the soft parts of her body.

It was supposed to be locked, but at that moment, the front door on the first floor slid open with a clatter.

The stairs creaked one after the next as a set of heavy footfalls made their way toward them.

"Is someone there . . . ?" echoed his brother's voice.

The girl caught her breath, silently gathering her belongings as the two of them hid behind the clothes rack. At this close distance, the girl's face shone with a mischievous glow. They continued to kiss each other, careful not to make a sound as they explored each other's bodies. Her skin grew warmer and warmer.

All of a sudden, the lights went out. The stairs creaked once more as his brother returned downstairs. He must have come to check why the lights were on in the fitting room, probably concluding that someone had simply forgotten to turn them off.

After the front door clattered shut once more, and they made sure that the visitor had disappeared off into the distance, the two of them burst out into laughter.

"Was that your brother?"

"Yeah. He's a total boor, and he's got a face like a potato. He doesn't know the first thing about women. He probably can't even put a kimono on or take one off."

"Does that mean you'll be taking over the store one day?"

"Who knows?"

One thing was for sure—his dim-witted brother certainly wasn't capable of doing so, Nowatari thought with disdain. His brother might have helped out with the accounting, but it was he who dealt with customers and explained how to use certain products whenever the store was crowded. It was as clear as day which of the two was better suited to inherit the business.

He had been absolutely sure of that, heart and soul—until the day he learned that his brother would indeed take over the store once he graduated from university.

At the time, his mother had reprimanded him for his dissipated behavior after finding a hairpin belonging to one of the girls whom he had invited over to the fitting room. When she casually mentioned that his brother would be making the rounds for the New Year greetings, he felt every pore in his body flare in anger.

"Why?! He doesn't even have a basic sense of color coordination!"

Lacking the self-assurance necessary to openly declare that he was the more talented of the two, he instead rained abuse on his brother.

His mother stared back at him with quiet eyes. "It's true, you have a knack for picking beautiful combinations. You did an excellent job the other day with the daughter of that assemblyman, picking out that under-kimono with the decorative collar to match that difficult obi she brought with her . . . But there's something cold about the way you look at other human beings."

"Wh–what kind of excuse is that?!"

"You love things of beauty, don't you? I can see it in the way you pick out clothes. But you don't have any familiarity with or take any interest in each individual customer's life, their struggles, their joys and dreams . . . You act like you're dressing a doll. When you see a customer, all you think about is expressing your own sense of beauty. That's not the job of a trader. That's why, no matter how unsteady his hand might be, your brother, who takes the time to empathize with customers, to help them choose a kimono that fits their needs and wants, is better suited to take over the family business."

Lost for words, Nowatari merely stared down at the tatami mat at his feet.

His mother, no doubt unable to read his thoughts, took him by the shoulders. "Listen, all I'm saying is that you aren't suited to *this* job. You definitely have talent, a special power that your father and brother lack. Find a way to make use of it . . . I'm sorry. I shouldn't have called you *cold*. *Calm* would have been a better word. You aren't moved by emotion. You're capable of ignoring things that other people would be too afraid to discard. Your gaze isn't cold. It's calm and reliable. And there will definitely be somewhere out there where you can make use of it." Biting her tongue, his mother stood up from her seat.

Ah, that was cruel, Nowatari thought as his younger self hung his head. His mother's criticism of his humanity had dealt him a sharp blow, one that hadn't just pierced flesh but had also shattered bone. At the very least, he would have preferred to have heard this from his father. He didn't want his mother to judge him with that probing scrutiny of hers.

"It isn't cruelty. It's love."

A woman's voice, high in pitch and warm to the ears, sounded behind him. He looked over his shoulder, finding a woman peeking out from behind a kimono hanging on a clothes rack.

He recognized this woman. She had a boyishly slim body and a short-cropped hairstyle, but her face was faintly sweet, reminiscent of a summer field. Her name began to spring to mind before getting stuck on the tip of his tongue. He couldn't afford to forget it, he thought with frustration.

The woman's face clouded over. "All you heard was the word *cold*, wasn't it? Your mother loved you, I'm sure of it. That's why she corrected herself and said *calm* instead."

"That doesn't change the fact that *cold* was the first word to come to mind for her. Everything after that was carefully thought out. But reflexively, instinctively, she rejected me."

Pierced by this old pain that had long lain unresolved, his body refused to move.

At that moment, the woman pulled him up with all her strength. "Love that comes from reason and

reflection is a lot more difficult and noble than in-
stinctive love."

"What do *you* know?"

"I *want* to understand. I made a vow to you." The
woman tugged at his hand, guiding him to the stairs.

It should have only been a few meters to the first
floor, but the staircase was long and narrow, disappearing into the distance. The woman took him
by the hand, the two of them twisting their bodies
slightly as she led him ever downward.

The light on the second floor faded into the background, and his vision grew dark. The steady rhythm
of their footsteps dulled his senses. Only the warmth
of the woman's palm felt real.

Had *he* made a vow like that?

He might have. But he had never interpreted it
that way.

A vow that the two of them would journey together on this dark path devoid of surroundings, that
they would forever be a pair in this world.

He *had* made such a promise.

Holding on faintly to the woman's hand, he continued to descend for what felt like a long, long time.

A WEAK LIGHT emerged beyond his feet. As he
continued down the steps, his vision opened up to
reveal a familiar Japanese-style house.

The corridor was wide, with a high ceiling, the floors and pillars polished until they gleamed. By the entrance, there was a *maki-e* partitioning screen decorated with a peony design made from gold powder, the black lacquer reflecting the light like running water. An old black telephone lay atop a lace vase mat.

No sooner did he realize that he was in his grandfather's house than he rejoiced. Its long, winding corridors, the creepy taxidermy birds in the tatami-floored rooms, strange household tools lying here and there—as a child, he had loved playing with his cousins in this house of wonders.

"Oh, what an adorable pair of lovebirds you two make."

A forty-something woman in a baggy cooking smock passed by holding a tray of dishes. Only when she narrowed her eyes in a warm smile did Nowatari notice that he was still holding hands.

He turned around and found a young girl with a bob cut staring at him wide-eyed. She looked to be almost elementary school age, her small, doll-like hand fitting comfortably around his.

His own hand, he realized, was no larger than hers.

A boy, laughing as he darted through the corridor, called out to him in a familiar voice: "Tetchan! Let's go exploring!"

Nowatari was struck with embarrassment at the thought that his cousin had seen him holding hands with a girl. Shame ran through his body, and he abruptly shook the girl's palm away.

The girl's mouth hung open in surprise. Nowatari felt a chill pierce his lower abdomen.

But they were going exploring. Exploring! His knees, sticking out from beneath his shorts, were itching to go.

The woman in the cooking smock, having left the tray of food in the hall, placed a hand on the girl's shoulder. "Tetchan, your uncle and the others have had a lot to drink, so I'm going to get some tea ready. Can I borrow your friend here to help for a minute? Go and play with the others for a while, okay?"

Okay? She had worded it as a question, but she was already guiding the girl to the kitchen, filled with the voices of women busy at work.

The girl glanced back at him two or three times before allowing herself to be led away.

Nowatari breathed a sigh of relief. *Now* he was free to go exploring.

He took off his socks and ran around the house barefoot, chasing after his cousin. He gazed at his grandfather's prized Japanese sword on display up in its alcove and listened to the ticking of his gilded pocket watch. Next, they did somersaults in the large tatami-floored room, played mock kung fu, and laughed until they were out of breath. It was fun.

For the first time in what felt like forever, his mind was clear.

But he couldn't relax. As much as he was enjoying himself, he couldn't shake the thought that he had forgotten something.

"Sorry, gotta go to the toilet," he said, darting back into the corridor.

He wanted to see what the girl was doing, even just to catch a peek. He hoped that she was smiling.

The men in the hall were completely drunk, their faces drooping like fairy-tale monsters. Their garrulous laughter and wide-armed gestures were more than a little scary.

One of them grabbed his head: "Ah, if it isn't Lord Tetsu! What are you up to, little man?"

He felt as though they were going to devour him, and so pulled himself away. "Have you seen a girl? She's around my height, with big round eyes. She was supposed to bring tea."

The men reeked of alcohol. "A girl? You're a bit young for that, aren't you? A girl!" The only response he received was a wave of laughter.

Strangely, the low, narrow tables in the hall were even longer than the corridor itself, stretching far into the distance. He continued to run past the drunken adults, but still he couldn't spot the girl.

He swallowed his impatience and darted into the kitchen. The huge women, at least three times his own height, were chattering loudly as they cooked at a tremendous pace. They were filleting, baking, steaming, frying, and juggling a neat assortment of trays and dishes that they ferried into the hall one after the other. As he looked up at the women's faces, various impressions tugged at his memories. This aunt was a cynic, this one mean-spirited. Those two were always criticizing one another to the other relatives behind each other's backs. A terrible premonition washed over his body.

Ah . . . The girl—where was she?

Rui wasn't at all a dexterous individual. She was a slow thinker and a poor talker, and even though she had worked in a restaurant and was used to preparing and serving food, she was neither quick on her feet nor particularly resourceful when it came to household chores. For anything that required a certain degree of finesse, such as cooking or sewing, Nowatari was the more capable of the pair.

He might have been able to deal with the older women, but if *she* was to venture into this bloodthirsty arena, she would surely find herself at the receiving end of their relentless domineering. As he timidly scanned the room, just thinking about how they would ridicule and prod her was enough to rend his heart.

"Hey! Where has the girl gone?"

But no matter how he called out, the women's

chattering continued like a tidal wave. A child's voice couldn't break past that unstoppable force.

This was bad. Whether she was in the kitchen or in the hall, she was undoubtedly afraid. He had to find her, quickly. They had to find a way out of this house, together. His impatience and shortness of breath reached their limit, and he stamped his feet in frustration.

"We made a promise! We have to stick together! *I'll* carry the tea! *I'll* help! *I'll* do a better job than her anyway! So give her back! Give her back!"

The scene in front of him wavered, the monstrous men and gigantic women shattering like glass. The next thing he knew, he was crying at the top of his lungs. Tears streamed down his cheeks, winding around to his neck and collar.

Suddenly, a warm droplet landed not on his cheek but on his temple, breaking near his hairline and soaking his scalp.

Then, his body woke up.

Slowly, he opened his eyes. As he blinked away the afterimage of that haunted house, he realized that he was lying in bed, staring up at a nondescript ceiling covered with pale cream-colored wallpaper. His body felt as heavy and as stiff as a boulder. The area around his temples was wet with a warm liquid.

A gentle voice called out to him, wiping the corners of his eyes: "You were crying, weren't you?"

No, he shook his head as he peered into her face.

Rui was lying beside him, dressed in her pajamas.

The sounds faded into the distance. Before he knew it, he had leapt to his feet, glancing around.

There was no forest. The mysterious trees had completely vanished, leaving only the couple's familiar bedroom. It must have all been a dream, he thought with relief, before immediately losing track of how it had even started.

In front of him was Rui, his wife, at the age that she was supposed to be. She rubbed her fingers, wet with his tears, several times against the blanket before inserting her hand under her pillow.

Teardrops spilled from the black, mirrorlike eyes staring back at him.

5

SHE BLINKED TO CLEAR THE WATER BRIMMING at the corners of her eyes, to restore her blurring vision and bring order to the objects bleeding into each other in front of her.

This brutal torture was no different from that which had befallen the legendary Monkey King Sun Wukong, Nowatari Rui thought. Her temples, the base of her nose, and the inner corners of her eyes all burned, while her head felt as though it were caught in an iron vice. The sense of reason that begged her to leave this person, and the body that gasped that it couldn't, were both inescapably her.

Why was she unable to stop loving this man, Nowatari Tetsuya, who didn't show her even the slightest ounce of consideration?

Why did the sight of this child stomping his feet, incapable of understanding the real problem here, fill her heart with a thousand disappointments? Why did it possess her with this senseless joy, this urge to cry, to feel sorry for him, to take him in her arms?

Nothing had been resolved. The moment that her husband laid eyes on her tears, his expression morphed into one of relief.

"Don't cry. Come on, let's go home. I'm sorry for making you feel lonely. We'll be together from now on."

Tetsuya spoke on the assumption that she had forgiven him. He didn't think of her as someone from whom he needed to ask forgiveness.

"You didn't want to quit your job at the restaurant, right? I understand. That was unreasonable of your uncle and aunt. I wish I could have talked them out of it. You can go back to work now, if you want. What do you think?"

Rui thought of Tetsuya as a gentle and clever man. Throughout the years, he had given her more than her own parents, whom she could barely remember, or her uncle and aunt, in whose home she had never been able to feel truly at ease.

Her uncle and aunt had never had much financial freedom, and so she had grown up helping out at the store from her midteens, leaving her with few opportunities to learn. She had never thought of herself as particularly smart, and she had always been filled with an inexplicable sense of awe by Tetsuya's intelligence.

That was why she was so happy when he showed her his study, the walls lined with books of all shapes and sizes, old and new, and encouraged her to read whatever she wanted. As she sat in front of those shelves, not knowing which to choose, Tetsuya pulled one of the books out, handing it to her. It was a collection of essays by a female author, written in a simple, easy-to-read style. The dishes described in it sounded so delicious that she could hardly wait to try cooking them for dinner.

As soon as she found a book that she liked, Tetsuya would tell her that this one was similar, or that this author was the exact opposite, naturally escorting her from work to work and so broadening her thinking. He was a good teacher, and a good giver too.

But for the longest time, she couldn't understand why her husband, who was so kind and clever, seemed always to be talking at cross-purposes with her. As her doubts piled up, her arguments would slip into some strange place, and she began to doubt whether he had ever truly understood her.

To begin with, Tetsuya was much more articulate than she was. In the middle of a conversation, he would often try to sum up her opinion. *This is what you mean, isn't it?* But whenever he did so, he would gradually move further and further away from whatever it was that she had actually been trying to say, and she would end up left with something that she couldn't control with words.

After a time, she realized that her tears must have stopped flowing at some point.

Tetsuya remained silent, merely pursing his lips at her, before glancing up at the ceiling and letting out a deep sigh. He scratched wearily at his neck, then reluctantly, almost unwillingly, opened his mouth: "All this time, you've been stressed out because we haven't had kids yet, right?"

Ah, yes. In the end, they had kept putting off having children. Rui blinked, staring back at him.

"Sure, if we had kids, you might not have ended up in this weird forest," he continued, his frown not letting up. "I never had time to think about all that, you see. I'm sorry for neglecting you, for always being busy with work. But things are looking up now. We've got a loan for the house and all that . . . If you want something to dote on, how about we get a dog?"

A dog? She had no idea what he was saying. How did a dog factor into all this?

He was the one who had always wanted a child. Ever since he laid eyes on a baby in a New Year's greeting card that he had received from his parents, he would say from time to time that living creatures were only complete when they had passed their genes on to the next generation. He had urged her to experience the mystery of childbirth, had urged her not to put it off until it was too late. And she, vaguely, had agreed with him.

However, there had been no sign of pregnancy even after six months of trying, and she began to wonder whether they would have trouble conceiving naturally. She suggested seeing an obstetrician, but Tetsuya stopped her, and the question of children was put on the back burner.

Tetsuya continued to talk: "I thought if we couldn't conceive naturally, we should just enjoy our lives together as a couple. But I guess this kind of thing is always harder on the woman. I wasn't considerate enough."

That wasn't what he had said before.

When she had told him that she was considering fertility treatment, he reacted with a look of disgust. "There's no use trying to find someone to blame," he said. Yes—looking back, they had always been talking at cross-purposes.

Something had been wrong this whole time.

This was much more serious than writing or not writing a novel, than going or not going to work, than having or not having children, but Tetsuya was forever unaware of it. In their relationship, it was always he who had the power to speak, and so any problem that he failed to recognize, no matter how serious, simply didn't exist.

It was a dead end.

No, this wasn't going to work. Not at all.

The iron vice gripping her brain prevented her thoughts from moving anywhere beyond that point. Rui held her head in her hands. The inside of her body turned black with sorrow. If she were smarter, she might have been able to point out exactly what was wrong with the two of them, to bring Tetsuya around and change the situation.

But she couldn't. She couldn't, and yet she couldn't give up either. She didn't want to live in this non-sensical place anymore. She wanted to go somewhere else, anywhere else.

The skin on her back burst into flame. The count-less impulses that she had kept folded up inside her overflowed like a dam breaking. A slithery sensation spread across her back, rampantly unfurling.

She once again sprouted green buds from every pore of her body, becoming a mass of greenery.

"I'm sick of your theatrics," Tetsuya mur-mured, without even trying to conceal his frus-tration. He leaned over, pressing his cheek against the headboard. "It isn't fair to use your hysterics as a weapon, to break down crying like that all the time. It's cowardly. When are you going to learn? It's impossible to hold a proper conversation if you don't even have a basic level of social ability. You women—well, it's kind of charming in its own way, and it's a shame that history never gave you all the right opportunities—but still, you're too quick to get emotional. You can't see that your lack of social skills is the root cause of all your problems, and then you misguidedly accuse *us* of discrimination and inequality."

Inequality . . .

Was *that* the source of her discomfort—in short, the inequality between men and women? Rui tilted her head, sinking deep into thought to the sound of rustling leaves.

Tetsuya, his tone languid, continued: "Our postwar democratic society is already equal and meritocratic. The strong survive and the weak perish. Sometimes, those who don't succeed are just unlucky, but most of the time, it's due to their lack of ability. And that's all there is to it. Everyone tries to make it sound more complicated than it really is. They don't have the courage to own up to reality."

The words, spoken quickly, took time to sink into her consciousness. She remembered the boy's back as he nodded to her in the fitting room, the kimono spread open on the clothes rack.

"Are you saying the reason you couldn't take over the family business was because you weren't as talented as your brother?"

A deep silence engulfed the bedroom—a silence emanating from Tetsuya.

His eyes had opened so wide that they risked tearing themselves apart. Through his clenched jaw, a pale anger flooded the room.

At last, he exhaled through his teeth, glaring at her with a bestial cast to his face. "Shut up."

It was a low, crushing warning.

She felt something writhing on her neck and back. "Why are you so angry?" she asked quietly.

But before she could even finish speaking, she was pushed violently away.

Her body bounced against the bed as she rolled over. In an instant, Tetsuya had inflated to twice his original size, transforming into a huge one-eyed monster covered in black bristles. He wanted to hit her, to control her, to hold her down. That huge, bloodshot eye radiated unrestrained hostility and spite. The next moment, as that black, mountain-like body raised its fists into the air, trees spilled out of her flesh with all the force of a flash flood.

Innumerable trunks and branches pierced through that huge eye, twisting and tightening as they lifted it into the air. Having fully ensnared that body, the trees began to exert further pressure. An eerie creaking filled the room as they squeezed its flesh, as they twisted its bones, until a scream, a man's voice, leaked out.

The pale flesh at the base of the trees, only barely

maintaining the outline of a person, let out a raspy voice: "Ah . . . So this is what it feels like to get angry. You know, you can't get angry unless you know you won't break. But I'm angry now. Really, really angry . . ."

Her pale flesh trembled, iridescent hairs erupting all over. A number of fist-sized spheres swelled beneath her skin, splitting the surface and opening up like fresh eyes.

Faced with that creature, with its soft hair and myriad eyeballs, Tetsuya forgot all about struggling and merely stared back. "Rui . . . Is that you?"

Those countless eyes, clear and white, watched him closely.

"Hey, let me down."

"No. I don't want you to hit me."

"I'm not going to hit you. I won't. Look . . ." Tetsuya lifted one of his arms into the air, showing her the mass of green leaves stretching from his ribs up to his neck. "See? I've got these now."

"Oh . . ."

"Let me down."

She didn't respond.

"We can't stay like this forever, can we?"

Blinking discontentedly, the rainbow-colored mass sank into the bed with Tetsuya, who was still ensnared by the trees. The white cotton sheets wrapped over them as their bodies pierced first the mattress and then the floor as they fell somewhere deeper.

When the sheets opened up again, they were sitting on the bed facing each other.

Rui, once again in her pajamas, gazed across at her husband, holding his knees with an expression of vague dissatisfaction.

Then, looking like he had just woken up from a dream, Tetsuya glanced up at the ceiling. "Hey, where are we?"

"The bedroom."

"I can see that. But this isn't our normal bedroom, is it?"

Was *that* the most important thing on his mind right now? She wondered why she had done as he had said and released him.

"You haven't apologized yet."

She could only barely put the sense of incongruity she felt into words.

But a bitter taste welled up in her mouth when she saw Tetsuya's unresponsive face.

"What do you mean? You did the exact same thing. There are no men or women in this weird place, right? You did that to me, and I did it back to you. So we're even."

But the problem wasn't about where or how many times an act of violence was perpetrated, and striking back the same way certainly wouldn't solve anything.

She felt as though her head was trapped in a deep

fog, and she pressed her hands against her temples. For some reason, she had thought that Tetsuya would apologize to her. She had assumed that he would understand what had just happened, that he would reflect on what he had done and say sorry. And yet it didn't even look like the utter dreadfulness of his actions had so much as registered with him.

She couldn't express herself well. She couldn't think properly.

"What's wrong?" he asked simply.

For him, everything had been reduced to a simple, banal question.

Rui stared back at him, her numbed tongue mouthing: *Apologize?*

Wasn't it common sense in this day and age just how awful it was to hit a woman? Wasn't he ashamed of himself? Every word that rose to her lips felt somehow inadequate. What exactly *was* this day and age? The word *normal* seemed like a pitfall. And was it really a question of *shame*? *She* was the one who had been faced with violence, *she* was the one who had been filled with disgust and repulsion, and yet the only words that came to mind were borrowed from somewhere else. In the first place, her plea for him to apologize didn't make any sense. If Tetsuya had been in her position, he would have told her that she was acting out of line, he would have denounced rather than implored her. He would certainly never have begged her for an apology.

Perhaps then, she should tell him that he was being inappropriate?

Changing the words *out of line* to *inappropriate* would greatly diminish the strength of the demand. Yet she couldn't articulate herself as directly as he could. She hadn't been brought up in that kind of culture.

Why was Tetsuya free to speak however he pleased, while her mind was crippled, her mouth practically sewn shut?

"Rui?"

"Wait here," she said, stepping down from the bed.

Tetsuya's eyes bulged. "Here?"

"Yes."

"Will you return to me as a lily a hundred years from now?"

"What?"

"No, it's nothing." His lips twitched slightly in amusement.

Rui stared at her husband curiously, then turned her attention to the large bookshelf along the bedroom wall. It was a solid fortress of wisdom, filled with thick, intimidating books that might spill off the shelves at any moment. From the shadows, a mass of vines coiled out invitingly.

She peered into those shadows, her fingers inter-twining with the vines.

Inside, the forest was expanding.

SHE FOUND HER as soon as she started paddling through the green dimness.

She was guarding a small, blue-tiled house in a round, open space beyond a break in the trees, set-ting up a table and chairs outside when she called out in greeting: "A visitor. How wonderful. No one ever comes here."

There was a pot of hot tea, some simple baked sweets, and a vase of pretty wildflowers lined up on the table.

"I've been waiting for him for so long now."

Her lover, it seemed was somewhere far away.

"I want us to live a happy life together."

Her voice as it tickled her ears was as clear as snow thawing in spring, free from even the faintest inkling of doubt.

"But he has an important job to do."

She had a pure, well-balanced face, a youthful neck, and lush, radiant hair. Her waist was so slender that a man might have been able to wrap his fingers around it, while her breasts had a solidity that could be seen even through her clothes.

"Once he's finished, he'll come back to me. Then, he'll take me away from here, he'll cherish me, and I'll give him sustenance. When he reaches out to me, I'll leave these branches behind and fall into his arms."

The scent of fresh apples and pears oozed from her body—a cool, sugary aroma of fruit almost on the verge of spoilage.

She had known her since she was a child, yet Rui stared at the woman as though only now meeting her for the first time.

"Won't you come out of this forest? Isn't there anything you want to do?" she asked.

"I'm already doing what I enjoy most—loving."

"If love is what makes you happiest, where's your partner?"

"Loving is *my* role. He has a wonderful task of his own that he has to finish."

"Why can't he love you *and* do that wonderful task of his at the same time?"

The woman smiled. It was a tolerant smile, the kind that all but said: *You don't understand yet, but you will, one day.*

Rui continued: "Hey, do we really like loving so much?"

"You love your husband too, don't you? You've built this ridiculous forest because you're desperately trying to reason with him, to accept him, to forgive him."

A damp breeze blew into the clearing, the surrounding trees rustling in unison. The undergrowth stretched taller, rising and swelling like dark-green waves. A solitary flower drooped helplessly, muddying the water as it moldered away. The wind had a familiar smell—a scent of cooking mixed with the aroma of sweetened soy sauce.

A voice, crying with all its might, rippled through the air. *We have to stick together!* he wailed. *Give her back! Give her back!* Beside the table, a pale mass of light in the shape of a child stomped on the ground in frustration.

"But you *were* happy when he said that," the woman laughed. "You were so happy you had all but decided to forgive him then and there."

"Of course I was happy. How could I not be, with the person I love trying so desperately to find me?" Rui said, squinting at the animated mass of light. "But no matter how much you love someone, there are some things you just can't forgive."

"Isn't that true love? The ability to accept your partner's weaknesses, their follies and cruelties? To forgive them?"

"If you can't reject, criticize, or seek to change what you don't like about someone, can you really call it love?"

"But love is supposed to be unconditional."

"That's why those who play the role of the lover are deprived of their sense of reason."

Rui thought back to the fitting room filled with all those colorful kimonos. The scene had left a bitter taste in her mouth. Her husband's younger self had assumed that only blind forgiveness qualified as love.

"Ah, this won't do."

Her disgust for Tetsuya overflowed, and she suddenly realized that the woman in front of her had become a blurry white shadow, like a watercolor painting dipped in water. She grabbed the woman's hand and tried to pull her out from the fog.

"Let's go. You said yourself that no one ever comes here. I don't want to forgive anyone anymore. When I find ugliness, I don't want to excuse it. I want to look it in the eye and talk about it."

"I wonder if that will work." The woman's voice wavered, wafting around her body like smoke. "It's painful to look each other in the eyes. Your husband is weak, sly. I wonder whether he can bear it? Is it truly love, having to endure each other like that?"

The woman and her sweet scent drifted around Rui for a short while, before fading away.

The next thing that she knew, the blue-tiled house was covered in plants, a mass of foliage crawling up from the ground to form a green mound. Thick and powerful branches had broken through the windows from inside, tearing through the collapsed ceiling as they spread their boughs and leaves. The chairs, the table, and the pretty wildflowers in their vase were all gone. The same unchanging darkness as before spread out in front of her.

Rui, overcome with a loneliness akin to saying goodbye to an old friend, blinked as a fresh wind swept through the circuits of her brain. Since her earliest memories, various parts of herself had been at odds with each other, but now the illusions of her mind and tongue were melting away.

When she stepped through the undergrowth and returned to the bedroom, Tetsuya was sitting on the bed, his back arched as he held an arm around one knee.

Wispy sprouts were budding all over him. His body having been taken over by the plants, he blinked his eyes every now and then, but otherwise he continued to stare at the small flowers growing amid the yellow moss that had popped up under his toenails.

The wildflowers in the vase earlier had been an illusion. There were no flowers in her forest. She stared at her husband's toes for a short while. It had been a long time since she had last seen a real flower.

"You were the one who became a flower, weren't you, Tetsuya?" she called out to him.

Her husband slowly raised his face. "I thought you weren't coming back."

"Was it that long?"

"I don't know. It's scary just waiting."

"It is, isn't it?" Rui nodded, stroking his back after a short pause.

The buds popping out between his shirt fibers arched softly beneath her fingers.

"Thank you for being so patient."

Rui climbed onto the bed. The mattress was lush with a thick blanket of grasses. She sat there, waiting for as long as it took for words to rise to the lips of her crouching companion.

"I never liked the way you tried to be so respectable all the time, even when you were at home . . . You always brought outside rules and customs inside with you."

The corners of Tetsuya's eyes twisted in a smile as he stared at the moss flowers. "We have a different view of marriage. I suppose we should have talked about all that from the get-go."

"Impossible," Rui said clearly. "I can't keep talking forever with someone who thinks he's so great just because he listens to what his wife says to him."

"You're still angry."

"*I'm* not the one who got angry."

"I'm sorry. I thought you were insulting me."

"There must be something wrong with your ears if you think throwing your own question back at you is an insult. And something wrong with your head too if you think it's okay to hit someone."

"I guess there *must* be something wrong with me then." As he murmured those self-deprecating words, Tetsuya's mouth began to loosen. The corners of his eyes wrinkled in laughter. He glanced across at her face before awkwardly averting his gaze. He was wearing a childish expression, one that she had never seen before.

"What's wrong?"

"I don't know. But it feels good. *This*."

"Oh?"

"I feel like I could become a mythical creature covered all over in eyeballs right now. A rainbow-colored one would be nice. It might change the way I see the world. It might even help me to write a new kind of story."

Rui tilted her head to one side, unable to grasp the point of Tetsuya's strange musings. A man with flowers growing from beneath his toenails. Was it possible that this person might be more capable of having a loving feminine side than she herself was?

"If you set your sights on it, you'll be able to pull it off sooner or later, don't you think?"

"Are you fine with your husband losing his man-liness?"

"I'd rather a mythical rainbow-colored creature

than a blood-eyed cyclops that tries to hit me. The crazy thing would be to accept you as you've been up till now."

"I see . . . I guess that's true . . ."

Tetsuya lifted his hand into the air, seemingly unconsciously. He gently scratched the back of his neck, particularly around the area thickest with buds. He blinked again and again, having lost his prior confidence and conviction, foreseeing change. His body relaxed, his watery eyes filling with emotions ranging from expectation to anxiety.

If she reached out, her fingers, she felt, might brush against this person's proud, moist soul.

The moment that she thought so, Rui found herself overflowing with a lust for him that she hadn't felt in a long time.

"Tetsuya, you're sexier now than you've ever been before."

"What are you talking about?"

He must have thought that she was joking around or being sarcastic. He pursed his lips in apparent doubt before creasing his brow and craning his neck as he looked up at the ceiling.

"To put this simply, we're in your dreams, right? Here, we're both plant monsters. We've abandoned our human bodies to free ourselves from the real world."

"I don't think so . . . Are you sure?"

"This place is separate from the outside world, right? A fanciful utopia where you can transform into whatever you want, where you can ignore all of history and culture if you feel like it. It's a fantasy world no more real than the rabbit hole that Alice dived into."

"What do you think is happening outside right now?"

She had no particular reason for asking that, but her thoughts were guided by the question.

Tetsuya's eyes opened wide, pierced by emptiness. "Outside?"

"I don't know either. But *you've* grown, Tetsuya. The forest might have spread further than you thought. We might just be two people dreaming together in our bedroom, but I'm sure it's all connected to the outside world."

"Spiritually, you mean?"

"I guess so?"

"I never used to believe in that kind of thing . . ."

Rui turned her attention to the bookshelves. As she gazed at the titles written on the spines of the many volumes, she remembered the scent of the woman who had disappeared into white mist. Just as the seeds of the forest had made their home within her, now too they had been sown inside him. There was probably nothing surprising about that. This bedroom was connected to the history and culture of the outside world, after all. These books were proof of that.

"Do you remember what I said, back when I first read *Tears*?"

"Hmm? Ah, right, I thought it was a little strange. Er . . . You said something about wishing *you* had a wife like that too." Tetsuya's eyes narrowed in amusement.

Rui nodded. "And do you remember what you said?"

"Not really."

"*Huh? That's how you read it?* That was what you said. And you laughed . . . That was what most surprised me. Because right up until that moment, I had been getting emotionally involved with the male protagonists of *all* the books in your study . . . I wanted to overcome all these hardships, to discover all these wonders. I wanted to go to places where no one had ever been before, to feel firsthand the mysteries of the world. I wanted to fight against cruelty and unfairness and discover the contours of my own life . . . It never occurred to me that those stories were all aimed at men. I just thought they were stories about people, people like me."

"What are you saying? Of course they're stories about people. No author cares whether they're read by men or women. There are plenty of readers out there like you who can sympathize with a character regardless of gender. There isn't a single author any-where who would be bothered by that."

Rui furrowed her brow. Something was off. She paused for a moment to collect her thoughts, then shook her head. "I reread a lot of the books I thought I liked, including yours. And they surprised me all over again. When I read them for the first time, from the main character's point of view, I hadn't really given any thought to how the women in those sto-ries could be so quick to forgive someone who tried to hit them, or how they could have sex with some-one they didn't love . . . But it's like you said. I'm a woman. Just like those sexually suggestive characters in all those books, the ones who become suddenly motherly and kind, who reward the hero for over-coming his difficulties, who have to *accept* everything as a fact of life. Those books taught me that the role of a beautiful woman was to *be* precisely that. And I enjoyed them without even realizing how wrong it all was . . . But going through them again, I couldn't believe I had let myself just go along with it all."

"Well . . . If you're going to complain, you should just read books by women authors. Don't whine about other people's bookshelves—build your own. You could read adventure stories by female authors with female protagonists. It isn't my fault if there aren't enough books like that on the mar-ket. That's on them. And besides, there are plenty of unrealistic depictions of men by female writers as well, so it's mutual. It's important not to encroach on each other's territory."

"If it's mutual, does that mean women are women, and so should be allowed to enjoy unrealistic depictions of men as much as they want?"

"That's what freedom of expression means. There's no use complaining to me about it."

It was Rui's turn to stare up at the ceiling. She began to swing her legs over the side of the bed as she sorted through her thoughts. Tetsuya continued to sit cross-legged in silence, resting his chin on his hands.

She suddenly realized that he was waiting for her to speak, without trying to summarize her thoughts for her as he usually did.

"But that's just like what you said about violence."

"Hmm?"

"If someone does it to you, you do it back to them . . . But if you just keep hitting each other, you'll both end up miserable. Before you know it, you won't even be able to move anymore . . ."

"Regulating expressions that are offensive to you is the first step toward discrimination."

"I'm not saying they should disappear. It's just, well . . . I want to read more stories where gender doesn't play into who the characters are or what they can do. They wouldn't have to encroach on anyone's territory . . . And just so you know, I don't

like that word, *territory*. Anyway, they wouldn't
have to be aimed specifically at men or women. It
could be like a neutral meeting place, where people can talk to each other normally. That would be
nice. If that's the middle ground, you could have
different gradations to appeal to the different tastes
of women and men."

Tetsuya, still resting his chin on his hands, stared
for a while at a point on the wall. "Maybe something
that passes the Bechdel Test?" he said at last.

"What's that?"

"It's a term in the film industry—basically, an
indicator to check whether a film is sexist or not.
There are three criteria: you need to have at least
two named female characters, they have to have a
conversation with each other, and that conversation
can't be about men."

"Why do you need a test for that? Isn't that just
normal?"

"You would think so. But not a whole lot of films
actually pass it. You would probably be surprised
how many famous classics don't." He paused there
for a moment, his tone turning bitter. "But even if
you tried to eliminate gender differences from your
works, the author is still going to be either a man or
a woman, and the society around them is still going
to have its own image of both genders. Eliminating
gender differences in your works would only give

you an unrealistic utopia. It would be dehumaniz-
ing, even."

"Even if there are still different gender roles in
society, why can't we just get rid of them for our
stories?"

Tetsuya pulled in his chin without responding.

Rui frowned, still not fully grasping his point.
"What's utopian about two women with names
talking about something other than men? It's the
other way around. If lots of movies can't pass that
test for some reason, then their narratives must be
incredibly narrow in scope. But reality is a whole lot
broader, a whole lot more varied . . . We could find
other forms that are more comfortable for the both of
us. I could become a massive cyclops; you could be a
rainbow-colored creature. We could even take turns
on different days. I'm sure there has to be a lot of pos-
sibilities out there. I want to read a story that scoops
them all up, not one that pretends they don't exist."

Tetsuya removed the hand propping up his chin,
placing it on his forehead as he sank into a long silence. Rui stared at the whorl of her husband's hair
and waited.

"Am I getting complaints from readers now?"

"I wonder? Maybe."

"If you want to read something that reconstructs
the definitions of big concepts like society or what it
means to be a human being, you should try science

fiction. And there are a lot of works of popular literature dealing with gender themes these days too. Let's take a look at some of them. Like I said earlier, you should make your own bookshelf," he said in his intellectual tone of voice before falling quiet once more. The corners of his lips twitched in hesitation. "And I'll think about what kind of story I can write next. Something completely different."

"I'd like that."

For a few seconds, Rui failed to understand the meaning of his proffered hand.

Tetsuya, his movements clumsy, carefully approached her. "We should talk more, the two of us."

Rui wrapped her arms around her husband's body and buried her cheeks in the budding neck of the tree. Her ear, pressed up against his chin, picked up a faint popping—the sound of a forest bursting into existence, one sapling at a time. She closed her eyes.

Her husband's forest would grow thick and engulf her own, taking on a completely new appearance. The forest would be renewed, suffering from new imperfections as it anxiously awaited the next cycle of fresh sprouts.

ON THE MORNING of the third Thursday of each month, Nowatari Rui climbed the stairs to the second-floor bedroom and ventured into the forest—filled now with orderly rows of tall conifers, the ground and tree trunks coated in moss and decorated with small flowers that resembled crushed sugar candies.

One by one, she collected the printouts from between the dark roots of the trees, arranging them by page number. When she had finished, she placed a hand on a nearby trunk, stroking its long, scaly bark and tracing a finger across its many protrusions and hollows. A mysterious sense of peace filled her heart, different from when she touched her husband's body or read one of his manuscripts.

The phone in her pocket began to vibrate. She slid her finger across the screen to accept the call. It was Shirasaki, informing her that she had just arrived at the nearest station. Rui answered in a whisper so as not to disturb her husband's writing, then removed her hand from the bark, soaked with the warmth of his body.

"See you soon," the writer's wife called out into the depths of the forest before quietly leaving the bedroom as she cradled the manuscript in her arms.

© Hisaaki Mihara

MARU AYASE has published seventeen books, many of which have been finalists for major awards in Japan. *The Forest Brims Over* was originally published in 2019. This is her first title to be translated into English.

© Taisuke Sato

HAYDN TROWELL is an Australian literary translator of modern and contemporary Japanese fiction. His translations include *Touring the Land of the Dead* and *Love at Six Thousand Degrees* by Maki Kashimada, *The Mud of a Century* by Yuka Ishii, and *The Rainbow* by Yasunari Kawabata.